A TOKEN'S WORTH

SPAWN OF DARKNESS

S. A. PARKER

A Token's Worth (Spawn of Darkness Series)

Copyright © S. A. Parker, all rights reserved.

This series is a work of fiction. Any resemblance to characters and situations is purely coincidental and not intended by the author.

Cover Images - Shutterstock

Gold vector created by freepik

❀ Created with Vellum

NOTE TO THE READER

This is book one in the four-part Spawn of Darkness series, written from Dell's perspective. It is a slow burn reverse harem romance with sensitive and taboo subjects, offensive language, sex slavery, explicit sexual content and violence; particularly as the series progresses. It contains subjective content which some readers may find triggering. Intended for an audience aged eighteen years and over.

CONTENTS

Prologue	1
Chapter 1	3
Chapter 2	8
Chapter 3	19
Chapter 4	31
Chapter 5	34
Chapter 6	48
Chapter 7	54
Chapter 8	65
Chapter 9	72
Chapter 10	84
Chapter 11	88
Chapter 12	92
Chapter 13	108
Chapter 14	124
Acknowledgments	137
About the Author	139
Spawn of Darkness Series	141

For Mum and Nana.
Thank you for showing me the true value of a woman's worth.

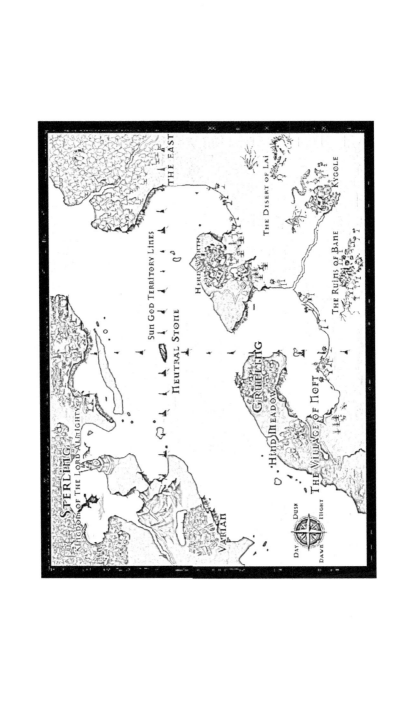

PROLOGUE

I could start my story anywhere, but I've decided to start it here. Mainly because it's the beginning of ... well, something.

It's cruel and uncouth, a bit fucking raw. It's the stuff people don't talk about because it makes them feel dirty or exposed. But this is how the world is for some. For me.

Imagine being stripped down to the bare bones of your existence, only to reinvent yourself in a way you don't recognise, or like. Would you hate yourself if you became a monster?

My life is certainly no fairy-tale. *This* is not a fairy-tale.

At times you'll cringe, and despite yourself, at times you'll get excited over my pain and suffering. Don't worry, I won't judge you. We're all the same to some extent. I'm the same. Sometimes I get excited over my *own* pain and suffering. Call me broken, call me a monster, call me whatever the hell you want. In your perspective, you'll be right.

But it's normal. To someone. To me.

I want for things I'll never have, and they aren't your regular wants. They make me question my moral aptitude, though not all the time. I'm no saint. Just don't analyse me because it'll probably send you in circles.

Also, I swear a lot. Pre-warning. It's a by-product of the way I see the world, and I see a lot of fucking. I do a lot of fucking. Not necessarily willingly.

That's not to say I don't enjoy it at times.

Welcome to the shit show that is my life. I'm not going to miss facts to protect your soul from the savagery. Sorry.

I hope you remember this apology later.

CHAPTER ONE

I've been taken against my will before, you're an easy target when you have the mark plastered on your motherfucking palm. But this morning, when five men corner me down a side alley that's usually void of people at this early hour, I'm not in the goddamn mood.

They're caped in the stench of expensive whisky. I mark them all ... fuck-knuckle one to five.

My mind's like a great big filing system. I forget nothing. *Nothing*. Sometimes, no ... most of the time, it's a curse. One I'm not sure how to cope with.

Fuck-knuckle one, tall with burly shoulders, plasters my body against the wall, hiking my skirt over my hips.

I should be used to being touched by unfamiliar hands. I'm not. It makes me feel filthy. Besides, this is not consensual. In fact, if we're counting consensual sexual encounters, then fuck me, I'd still be a virgin.

It's best to stay calm. They tend to beat you less when you're calm. That, and there's no point screaming for help. Nobody will come. Except to watch the free entertainment.

Instead I'm whimpering, and I just can't seem to stop.

I barely recognise myself.

The bag of fruit I've been carrying drops to the ground, the apples and oranges scattering like the last threads of my composure. When he pushes himself inside me, I'm dry as a goddamn drought in there. Not that it slows him down. He thrusts into me, pulling my hair so hard I can't close my mouth while the other four watch on, cocks in hand. Sadistic pricks.

The tiny part of me that enjoys this public exhibition is traitorous, but at the same time I'm relieved when my vagina finally comes to the party and creates her own moisture. Now it doesn't hurt so much. Though it does little to salvage my crumbling mental composure.

The man inside me groans. "She's wet, she's enjoying it!" He thrusts harder as his hand comes around and gropes at the slickness between my legs.

I wish I could cry at times like this. Instead I'm screaming. Screaming for more.

I fucking hate myself for it.

Yet again, my body and mind are at war with each other.

It's wrong in so many ways. But it's me. It's what I'm used to.

This is my fucked-up reality.

He swings me around, pushing me to my knees and skinning them in the process. Fuck-knuckle five forces a penis that tastes like it's been languishing in his sweaty underpants for the past six months into my mouth. I reflex gag. He goes harder. "Take it, bitch! And keep those fangs in check!"

I could bite down anyway, but the punishment would be death by guillotine. I consider. Yeah, pretty fucking tempting.

I'm furious with my vagina when the orgasm almost tears me in half. She likes it rough, back stabbing bitch, and I swear it turns them all savage—all wanting to rip their own glory from me as well. Which they do.

My vagina may be having a party down there, but my mind's scrambling for purchase. It was so much easier when I could switch off and let them get on with it. Now I'm all fucked up and I have no idea how to claw my way back.

I'm not sure when I pass out, have no idea if it stopped them. I think not because when I wake, sprawled along the ground and dangerously close to a puddle of piss, my rear end aches. Arseholes. Right now I'm glad I don't have a uterus, because that would be some funky cocktail baby.

There's a token in the dirt, payment for my services they didn't ask to hire in the first place.

A single token.

Granted, it could buy the girls and me three loaves of bread every day for a month in these parts—something other than cum to fill our stomachs during the long day shifts.

I stare at the token, smothered in filth, lying on the ground.

Not today.

I spit on it and leave it in the dirt.

Walking is difficult—I think I'm broken inside. Slowly, I make my way through town, trudging through mud, faeces, piss … passing other whores, faces caked in powder and rogue, coal staining their eyes and creating a semblance of beauty to cover the fact that they're empty. Barren. Broken.

Caped in red—the damning colour of females—they hail men still drunk on last night's juice into their whore lairs. Some of them even beam their tattered smiles while they're at it.

I trudge through narrow streets plagued with deep shadows and crammed with dingy shops, derelict living quarters and whore houses. There's an abundance of red washing hanging on the lines that zig zag across the barely visible sky; scarlet ghosts in the scarce morning light.

There's no room to move in this town. Barely room to breathe.

I pass the shop that always smells like freshly baked scones no matter what time of the day it is. The scent reminds me of the comforts I once had.

I think of my mother.

I try not to think of the last time I saw her.

The air is brisk, pebbling my exposed skin and highlighting the many scars I'm marred with, turning them an odd shade of silver. I run the pad of my index finger over the one on the palm of my hand. The one I can't escape from. Ever. The air I puff is milky white, but the cold is akin to the other sensations I'm feeling right now, crumbling my reinforcements I'd convinced myself were sturdy.

A man stumbles past, a whore at his side, his hand dancing up her skirt. He leads her towards a door, perhaps to a bed that's nicer than the one she sleeps in regularly.

I see her fake smile, the disdain in her eyes.

She'll likely enjoy the softness of his sheets—may even pretend he's courting her so she can get off easier. Been there, done that. It leaves a bad taste in your mouth.

The air becomes thick as I pass through the fish market—churning with women too weathered for the vagina trade, up to their elbows in fish guts and gore.

Few spare me a second glance. The ones that do wield distant eyes, as though they've seen this before. Been in my position. They quickly avert their gazes, and I'm not offended. For them, it wouldn't be worth the punishment. The loss of a limb, a public whipping …

Death.

A couple of dogs, flea ridden and skeletal, maul each other over a bone half buried in mud. The smaller of the two begins to mewl, backing away and bowing to the larger.

Lips pulled back, baring sharp teeth that drip with

desperation, the victor walks past me—prize in jaw, headed for a narrow side alley where he can enjoy his meagre meal in peace. I spot the decomposing human hand dangling from the end of the bone.

I stop, ankle deep in filth, watching the dog feast on the remains of someone's lost capabilities.

This is my life. This is my world.

My world.

I've had enough.

CHAPTER TWO

It's not until I near the cliff edge, the horizon fanning out before me, that I realise what I'm about to do. I can't go back anyway … perhaps I'm just grasping at testicles here, but I left the apples and oranges I got from the pre-dawn market on the motherfucking footpath. Not that they would've stayed there long, but to go back without them would be a one-way ticket to the whipping posts. Fuck that. I'm not getting whipped for apples and oranges. Kroe's had others whipped for less.

We're just numbers to him, replaceable. Even though we pay the bills for his opulent lifestyle. All the customers need to do is slide into our cunts and Kroe gets a token for every ten minutes taken. *We* get a roof over our head, though it's best not to get attached to the other girls at the establishment. They come in as quickly as they go out, for one reason or another. Some reasons far more sinister than the guillotine.

Often the mind deteriorates faster than the body. Exhibit A.

We keep each other warm at night, it's a nice comfort and

it gives us a small sense of belonging and sisterhood. The rest of the time I barely acknowledge them, even in secret. Instead, I have internal conversations with my vagina. She's an interesting confidant, though not always sensical.

I know what you're thinking, but I'm not *that* crazy; just fucking repressed, like all the women these days.

Not that any of that matters now.

When I kneel on the grassy band at the edge of the cliff, I wince at the biting sensation, certain there's gravel buried in the fleshy cuts. I don't care enough to inspect them.

Life wasn't always so vicious for females—a girl whispered something similar to me once, before she was beheaded publicly for speaking ill of our lot in life. Perhaps her vagina wasn't very conversational because she just couldn't keep her mouth shut. Instead, she trusted all the wrong people, an unforgiving lesson not to speak ill of our Lord Almighty, King of the World, bringer of fuckery, arsehole extraordinaire and his pure white fucking feathers.

The waves crashing against the rocks below echo my tumultuous mind as my hair whips at me from all angles. I hate this pain in my fucking heart.

It's this moment, when the sun peaks over the horizon and night begins its subtle fade to day, that words of an ancient tongue come to mind. I'm not sure how I know them, nor do I know what they mean, which is strange because I remember everything. Nonetheless, I speak these words to the dawn, as the new day begins to rouse from night's embrace.

"Gleitz adorn, de mel te heist. Sevana ta lein."

My skin prickles and a sudden wave of heat washes over my body. I curl over, gasping for air. The tiny hairs on the back of my neck begin to rise—something shuffles behind me...

I straighten, turn, and freeze.

This is not my fucking day.

My insides coil with dread, my lungs forgetting how to process air momentarily. I'd bang them back into action, but my arms are hanging at my sides like a couple of limp dicks at an orgy. Useless.

Standing before me are three immortal, High Fae males. My vagina bows, but I do no such thing, even though I recognise these men from artistic depictions and verbal embellishments. They're donned in gleaming metallic god gear and wearing an air of bravado.

Rightly speaking, I should be kissing their feet right now.

Dawn, Night, and Day—three of the four Sun Gods, second only to our overriding King. Though apparently, the Sun Gods are just as sinister as our savage Lord Almighty, which means I'm probably about to have penises plugged into my every available orifice then be chopped into bite sized pieces and thrown to the megalodon's. Not that they would struggle with eating me whole, but that's not the point. The point is, I'm fucked.

I bare my canines, then instantly catch myself, reining the bastards back in before the Gods take it upon themselves to yank them out for my feral insubordination. Kroe did that to a girl once, it wasn't pleasant to watch.

They look at each other with confused expressions, then back at me.

"You summoned, and we came," Day states, with a hard gleam in his eye.

I ... what?

Night snickers. "Came ..."

Day gives him a filthy sideways glance. "Really?"

Night shrugs. "That's the best you could come up with after two hundred and fifty years of wish drought? 'You summoned, and we came'?" Night impersonates Day's deep voice.

Day clears his throat, squaring his broad, throw-my-legs-over-while-he-fucks-me, shoulders. I internally slap my face. Shut up, vagina. Keep your thoughts to yourself.

Dawn cocks a brow.

I stare at them, confused, and not wanting to speak because I'd likely lose three limbs instantly. They'd probably just magically fall off. What an existence that would be. Kroe would sit me on a specially designed chair and let men fuck me all day, every day. I'd probably die choking on a penis. What a shit way to go.

"You can speak, mortal," Dawn drawls, his gaze branding me.

Wow. Okay, I can speak. That's ... not what I was expecting. "What are you all doing here?" I croak, because it's a valid question. They're immortal. *High Fae*. What's more, they're fucking *gods*! This land of squalor and poverty is for the *mortals—lesser* beings. People like me.

They look at each other and shake their godly heads, apparently not getting it. That's unfortunate—obviously their brains don't amass to the impressive packages they appear to have between their legs. Not that I'm looking, of course, even though my vagina's trying to wiggle out to catch a peep, but those leather god pants peaking through the armour leave *very* little to the imagination.

Day answers. "You called upon us for a wish? With the ancient words we thought were lost to the world?"

I stare at him, eyebrows raised. What the fuck is he on about?

"You would usually only get one of us?"

I shake my head. Nope, no clues.

He sighs, and Night intervenes. "You just happened to reach us right on the crossover from night to day, and smack in the middle of dawn. It's a grey area, so we've all been summoned." He glances at the other two. "Until they fuck off, anyway."

Day sneers at him. "Watch yourself, Night. Last I checked you were losing some of your touch. That's what happens when you spend your days fucking and not training."

Ouch.

"That's not why I'm losing my touch and you know it. We're all losing it, you included, arsehole."

Day bristles and I almost wet my panties, because he's a big, scary god with obvious anger issues.

Wow. Seems like I've walked right into the middle of a family dispute. I'm not sure if I'm expected to mediate, but I don't think I'm up to the challenge right now.

"And we'll continue to lose it, especially if you scare away our first wish in almost two hundred and fifty years," Dawn states, which starts an all-out bickering contest from the other two.

I get the feeling Dawn's the only one amongst them with any sense. So much for ancient wisdom. Talking about sense, I have enough of it to know not to get further involved with these so-called gods.

"Actually, I made a mistake," I yell over their ramble. They look blankly towards me, as if they'd entirely forgotten I was here. Bastards. "You can all kindly fuck off. Sorry for the inconvenience." I give them a 'shooing' motion with my hands. I'll probably get skinned alive for that, but the alternative predatory god gang-bang isn't that appealing, either.

Shut your labia, vagina, you're supposed to be sleeping off your trauma.

These men are big and scary, and from my knowledge, centuries old and powerful. I've got enough men with egos in my life, and if these guys are closely associated with King Sterling, as is rumoured, no fucking thank you.

Well, fuck me, now I well and truly have their attention.

Three pairs of eyes look my way—powder blue, molten amber, and deep navy. It's making my insides quiver in fear, and maybe a little arousal, though I choose to ignore that. Fucking vagina's a menace. I lift my chin, just to be sure I look strong, confident, and unaroused.

Dawn laughs. "No, mortal, that's not actually how this works. You see, your words just created a binding contract between us."

Ahh...

"Fuck that, unbind it." That's the obvious solution to this scenario. I don't want to be bound to them, and I'm sure they don't want to be bound to a Lesser Fae *female.*

"Impossible," Day says, taking over the reins in his booming voice that makes me feel about as small as my underappreciated nipples. "You can't unbind from us, not unless you're prepared to die in the process. We will not die because we're immortal Fae, but you will wither into nothing but a small pile of worthless dust."

Wow, so Day's an arsehole. Duly noted.

"That's a bit harsh, what about buyer's remorse?" A valid question, considering I unwillingly and unknowingly entered into this godforsaken contract.

"Nobody ever has buyer's remorse—look at us." Night sweeps his hands from the top of his black, sculptured god wear, gesturing all the way down to his shit kicking boots. He looks as badass as I wish I felt right now. But I *don't* feel badass. Mainly because I'm stuck in the presence of three gods who have bound themselves to my soul, and I'm almost certain I don't get this supposed *wish* for free, because these guys aren't exactly pure. Not from what I've heard.

"*I* have buyer's remorse," I state, taking a step back, which brings me extremely close to the cliff's edge.

"Well suck it up, little mortal. You're stuck with us," growls Day, and I almost wet my prostitute-panties.

They take a step forward.

There's a sudden flash of white. The three of them curse colourfully as I'm hit with another wave of warmth. "Oomph."

I'm curled over, gulping air, when I see a new set of feet standing before me. No ... "Why the fuck is there *another one?*" I gasp, recovering.

Dusk, the fourth Sun God, dressed in golden god wear, is all gleaming perfection. Nobody should look that good.

"Great question," Day sneers, baring his canines at Dusk.

"I wasn't expecting a welcoming party, I would've brought snacks." Dusk's voice is deep and husky, and he has a wicked gleam in his eye when he looks me over. My traitorous whore vagina's sniffing the air like a rogue bitch in heat.

"So ... why *are* you here?" Night asks Dusk, though Dusk doesn't respond. Instead, he looks straight past Night, to Day, who's watching him like a predator on a hunt for a dusk feast to feed his starving family.

"Why the fuck are *you* here, Day?" Dusk growls.

Night rolls his eyes and intervenes, stepping between the two. "Because she made her wish right on the threshold this morning. *So*, why are *you* here?"

Dusk shrugs with a face all nonchalant and perfect looking. "It's dusk somewhere in the world at the moment."

The other three glare at him.

"What? I'm not missing out on the first fucking wish in over two centuries just because she had a moment at the wrong fucking time of day. Nope. Count me the fuck in."

"You say fuck a lot," I interject. Not that I can talk—my inner monologue consists primarily of the word fuck.

Dusk shifts his attention to me, which, I'm not going to lie, makes me weak at the knees. My vagina's practically purring and needs a decent talking to, because her lack of self-preservation skills leave a lot to be desired.

"That's because I fuck a lot." He throws me a wink.

I shiver a little. The bitch between my legs wants to pee all over him and mark her territory. She's so unladylike sometimes.

They aren't at all how the stories portray them to be. They don't seem all that *godly,* and they haven't killed me yet which is strange, because I've spoken out of turn eight times already. I'm confused. They seem more interested in bickering and growling like animals than running the world. Not that I think that's their job ... that's the King's job, but still. How did ancient men become so petty? Immortality must be boring.

"Why are you looking at me like that?" Dusk asks, brow furrowing.

Ok, so my head's cocked to the side and I'm studying him intently, as if he has five arms and a penis protruding from his forehead. I straighten and compose myself. "Nothing. You guys just aren't what I expected."

"What were you expecting?"

"I don't know. I didn't expect my body to still be intact and functioning at this point, though." And by 'body' I mean my vagina, but I'm not going to bring that up right now and put ideas in those ancient heads of theirs. All eight of them.

Dusk arches a perfect golden brow. "Just say the word and I'm more than happy to do a quality control check on *just* how functional your body still is." His voice is laced with a husky undertone that sends tingles straight to my randy vagina. Where's a chastity belt when I need one?

"Dusk, goddamnit, I know you have a taste for Lesser Fae flesh but please, keep it in your pants for one goddamn sun cycle," Day spits.

"You're really damning those gods, aren't you?" I say,

before I can rein my fucking mouth in. I swear Day's canines lengthen. Scary.

"We are the fucking gods. And believe me, we're already damned."

My alarm bells are ringing, even though my vagina's ears are perked and she's snatching at thin air. She has a mind of her own and doesn't know what's good for her. If getting lumped with these primal High Fae Gods, who will probably condone torture like I've never experienced before, is my B option, I don't want it. Sorry, vagina.

I'm fucked either way. Do I want the pain drawn out, or over in a flash?

Easy answer.

"Right, well, good for you lot," I say, in the merriest voice I can muster. "I've decided I want these wishes after all."

They look at me quizzically, but it's Night, all dark and mysterious, who answers. "Wish, little one. Not wishes."

I look at him flatly, because he's being a slippery sausage whether he realises it or not. "No ... wishes. *Four* of you are here, that means I get four wishes."

They study me as if I've just grown a penis. I don't bother telling them that I won't be needing all four, but I like to exercise my rights as a living mortal. Now that I have some, that is.

Dusk is the first to answer, grinding his jaw as if he's truly pissed that I called them out on the shit deal they were offering me. "Fine. Four linked fucking wishes. I'll take the first one. What's it to be, mortal?"

The waves crashing at the bottom of the cliff send up plumes of sea spray that dance over my skin and make it pebble. I straighten my shoulders, trying to look a little badass even though I feel utterly deflated. Despite my small victory, my body still aches and I smell like a cum dumpster. Like I said, I've had enough.

"I want to be fearless."

Dusk clears his throat. "No can do. I can't permanently change your makeup. You're born with what you're born with." He may sound like sultry sex on a stick, but he has a crude gleam in his eyes that suggests he has a taste for control. I've become good at reading men.

"What about temporarily?"

Dusk's frown deepens as he studies me, golden eyes smouldering. I'm sure girls go weak at the knees for him, right before he cuffs them and fucks them seven ways sideways until they're screaming out the safe word. "Yes … I'm able to do that."

Great. No time to lose my testicles now. "Do it then," I say in my best 'fearless' tone, because I like to play the part seamlessly.

They shuffle about me as Dusk and I hold each other's gaze. "Is that your wish?"

Swallowing the lump in my throat, I nod. "Yes."

His jaw stiffens, a muscle along it twitching as he clenches his fists. "Then say it," he snaps.

Fuck me, I bet his bedroom talk is on point.

"I wish for you to make me fearless for five minutes." Why five minutes? Because it seems High Fae are slippery, and momentarily could be interpreted any way he wants to interpret it. I've been fucked enough today, I'm not interested in it happening again.

He exhales and closes his eyes, drawing a deep breath then opening them again. They appear to blaze a deeper hue of gold as a warm wash envelopes me. I feel a metaphorical weight lift from my shoulders.

I close my eyes, straighten, stretch my arms and crack my neck.

Fuck yes. That's what I'm talking about. I'm fucking invincible.

I open my eyes and smile, catching the glares of four very serious looking gods. I smile wider, because this is the bees-fucking-knees. I can do anything.

Dusk catches my gaze and I throw him a wink, because I'm totally badass right now. "Thanks."

I saunter a step backwards, towards the edge of the cliff that no longer seems so frightening. But sauntering like a badass hurts like a motherfucker because my arse definitely took a beating today.

The four males converge, nostrils flared. They probably want a go too, sadistic pricks.

Another step and I reach the edge. I don't even look down before I throw myself off backwards. I'm fearless as fuck, and like I said, I'm done.

I free-fall, spinning so I'm falling face first.

I'm flying.

The thought flutters through my mind that this is the best way to go, because right now I feel more alive than ever. But then I hit something hard and warm, halting my progress towards the rocks below.

I'm swept into a storm that sends me tumbling into a sea of white and out of consciousness.

I really hope this is fucking heaven.

CHAPTER THREE

I'm pretty sure I'm not dead when I come to. Fuck it. Not that I open my eyes immediately, but I can hear two males bickering a short distance away.

I strain to hear what they're saying, trying to ascertain as much as I can about my surroundings before I make it obvious I'm no longer passed out, because I may need to formulate an escape plan.

"Well, that was a fucking disaster. Somehow, you just broke the law, twice." Day's voice makes my vagina think dirty thoughts, because it's more frightening than ever.

"You would've done the same, cockhead. Admit it." Dusk, and he just said 'cockhead'. Wow. I thought I was immature.

"I'm not saying I wouldn't have, I'm just saying this is a disaster that shouldn't have been possible in the first place. We might get skinned alive for it." Day again. My vagina's panting. Randy tart.

And who would skin them alive? They're fucking gods!

"He won't find out." This comes from a different voice, I think it's Dawn's. "I'll hide her in my territory."

"Fuck off." Dusk again. He has that deep husky voice

that probably lures even the most prudish virgins out of hiding, though I doubt there's many of them about these days. He sounds like he's only a few feet away from me now. "You don't get to keep her. My drako needs a friend. I want her."

"No. If the old territory lines still applied she would technically be under my protection anyway. There's no point in arguing with me over this." What the hell is Dawn talking about?

"Well they *don't* still apply, and we all know why that is, so moving the fuck on. I've got an antisocial drako with attachment issues. The toddler stage is killing me, and she still has another thirty fucking years of it to go. She needs a woman's touch…"

What the fuck is going on?

Day scoffs. "Doesn't she get exposed to a new woman every day, and hate every single one of them? Your argument's falling flat, arsehole. The mortal pet will come to the Day Kingdom with me. Case closed."

Yup, I'm definitely not dead. Unless I died and went to hell. In which case I'm fucked, literally, because I'm pretty sure at least two of the four Sun Gods are sadists. If only I wasn't so good at reading men.

"She's not a pet," Night rumbles, in his seductive bedroom voice that heats my nether regions.

"She owes me payment for her wish, so you can all fuck off. She's mine." Dusk again. And payment? I knew I wasn't getting something for nothing! Slippery sadistic Fae Gods!

"Yeah well, she owes us all, in case you've forgotten. You'll just have to share the mortal pet with the rest of us until our contracts are paid out." Day again. I owe them all? But I only got one wish! I'm not liking the way this conversation's going.

"I'm okay with sharing. I like to share." Night. Of course

he's okay to share—he's the sultry seductive type. He probably has his own harem.

They *all* probably have their own harems!

Fuck. That.

I'm out.

I snap my eyes open, quickly taking in my surroundings. Which are ... *disorientating.* The air about me is shimmering with overwhelming light, creating millions of teeny tiny rainbows and suffocating my bearings.

Woah, head spin.

What the fuck?

"By the way, she's awake."

"Could've said that earlier, Dawn!"

"Nah."

My eyes try to adjust, unsuccessfully. How long have I been out for? Fuck knows, but I need to get away. I need to run. Now. Not that I can see the ground, but hey, at least I can feel it. I can also feel my broken bits throbbing inside me.

I stumble to my feet, shielding my eyes from the brightness of this weird little world, fumble forward a few steps and bang into something firm and warm. Thick arms wrap around me.

Ugh. This really is *not* my day.

"Where do you think you're going?"

Dropping my hand, I blink in the direction of Dusk's voice, almost two heads higher than me. My vagina likes them tall. Calm your labia, twat.

He slowly comes into focus, those tiny rainbows coagulating to form the Sun God holding me captive.

I clear my throat, because all that golden skin, golden hair, and golden *everything* is disarming at such close proximity. High cheekbones and a square jawline to boot, not to mention that chin dimple. Even my wounded sexual appetite has awakened. Down girl.

"Ahhhh, home. I'm going home," I state in a fearless tone, even though I'm no longer fearless. Doesn't hurt to fake it.

He shakes his head, ruffling his curls. "You lost the right to make that choice when you threw yourself off a cliff. Now, unfortunately for you, you're our responsibility." He frowns, and I can't be certain, but his eyes seem to darken as his arms tighten around me ever so slightly. "Stupid mortal."

"I'm my *own* responsibility, thank you very much!"

I wriggle to escape, but he spins me around, large hands wrapping around my bruised wrists. I wince and his hold loosens. Footsteps approach and I'm faced with three more gods—three more judgmental glares sharpening from the sea of rainbow. They dip to the hands grasping my wrists, then back to my face.

My lungs deflate, my body becomes slack, because these men ... although they're intimidating with physiques built for the battlefield and surely not everyday use, they're stunning. My vagina and I agree on something, for a change.

Each of them is unique, physically sculptured to represent their time in the sun cycle.

Dawn, auburn haired with molten amber eyes and honey skin. He towers over me, as they all do. He's pretty, with high cheekbones and fine hands. I'm also fairly certain he's a sadist. Even though he's calmly composed, there's something about the gleam in his eyes that I recognise from past experiences. I try not to judge a book by its cover, though I'm usually right. Not to jingle my own bell or anything, but ... ring a ding ding.

Then there's Day, all platinum hair and chiselled beauty—the way I would depict a god if I were to draw one. He's the tallest, yet perfectly proportioned with broad shoulders and a tapered waistline. Day likes control, I can see that already. Somehow, I've pissed him off, because he's looking *angry* right now, staring at me with a glare heavier than a two-tonne penis standing to attention, and I don't particularly want to learn the consequences of *said anger*. My vagina does, but I'm sending her to the sin bin. She needs some time out before she digs us into a hole writhing with godly penises.

I shift my gaze to Night with his tousled ebony hair, olive skin, full lips and eyes a rich tone of cobalt blue. He's looking at me like he wants to devour me whole, and hell, it's kind of working.

Wait ...

Fuck. I'm surrounded by four gorgeous gods who want to keep me as their pet, and I've just lost my way out ... not that I know where the hell we are right now. All I can see are rainbows and sexy Sun Gods.

I jerk myself out of Dusk's grip, right into the middle of the circle. "I refuse to be a part of your harems!" I speak with conviction, my head held high and shoulders back, because posture is important, especially when you're at least two feet shorter than the four gods boxing you in.

"What the fuck is she talking about?"

Shut up, Dusk. I'm trying to have an internal conversation with myself.

Fists clenching, they take small steps towards me. My palms feel sweaty and I don't know where to look. I'm used to attention, but this ... this is something else entirely.

I need to get out of here.

Seeing a gap between Dusk and Day's legs, I go for it, feeling super badass even though I only make it two feet before I'm pinned to the ground by one of them, the jarring action causing me to hiss in pain. At least the grass is soft. Well, I think it's grass. It smells like grass, but grass isn't usually made from bright little rainbows ...

A pair of hands grab my wrists and holds them firmly above my head. I kick my legs in a floundering attempt to escape, gain a small amount of traction before they, too, are pulled out from beneath me and pinned in place.

"Let me the fuck go!" I yell, exercising my newfound liberties.

"She thinks we're taking her..."

Was that Dawn? Why did he sound so concerned? And yeah, I'm not stupid, I know what this is. My vagina's excited, even from over there in the sin bin, but *I'm* a fucking wreck.

"Let me go, or I'll punch you fuckers in the dicks!" I scream, inhaling a mouthful of shiny, rainbow grass and gagging, though it's nowhere near as bad as choking on a penis.

Someone pulls at my corset from behind, swiftly unlacing it. I squirm, putting everything I have into fighting these four bastards off. Fuck this. There's no way I'm getting gang banged for the second time today. No vagina, I didn't ask for your opinion.

"Let me go!" My body jerks around in a very unladylike manner, likely causing more internal damage, but fuck it. Hands press onto me, stilling me in place, and now I'm growling like a feral beast.

Fuck men, fuck them all.

Another hand moves deftly across my back, down to a particularly tender spot. I wince and arch my back, difficult given my current position.

"What's all this from?" Day asks, followed by a few muffled hissing sounds.

Savages.

"None of your goddamn business," I growl.

"What did she say?"

"No idea."

Next thing I know my skirt's being hiked up from my ankles. I try to squirm away, unsuccessfully. Arseholes.

I can't do this. I can't fucking do this again.

"Somebody needs to do something, she's losing it."

"Not unless it's necessary," Day snaps, running his fingers over the scars around my neck. "It'll just confuse her more, and we can't waste the power."

Cryptic bastards.

The other hands don't stop until my skirt's bunched up around my waist and my vagina's drooling. I want to slap her silly for it. There are a few harsh intakes of breath followed by some crude yelling in a foreign tongue. It's about now I'm ready to throw myself off that cliff again.

My skirt is rolled back down without any unsanctioned prodding. Strange. Maybe they were scared away by the scent of my earlier gang bang. Ha! Small wins.

I'm rolled over and suddenly Day is all up in my face. At least he's not inspecting my abdomen. I like to keep *that* scar hidden when possible.

"Who did this to you?"

He's practically snarling, which is strange considering he's likely done worse to women before. Hell, they probably asked for it too, and moaned in orgasmic harmony the entire time. He seems the type.

"*Who?*"

I ignore the question, exercising my free will by folding my now released arms over my chest and closing my eyes. "Bossy Fae bastard."

"Fucking hell. I can't." I hear him rise and stalk off a few steps.

"Why don't you just fucking compel her?" Dusk yells.

That piques my interest enough for me to crack my left eye open.

Day folds his arms over his chest, making the muscles on his biceps bulge. "I'm not compelling her. Night?"

Yeah right, call upon the seductive one.

Night closes in on me just as I open my other eye. I glare

at him. If I'm going to survive this, if I'm going to convince them to let me go, I need to stand my ground. If they think I'm going to be too much trouble they'll lose interest in keeping me and my vagina as a pet.

Night tugs me slowly into a sitting position then runs a hand up my spine. My corset knots back together, shoving my breasts up high. Hey there, ladies.

"What's your name, pet?"

"Krystal," I say, silently praying that I'm not going to burst into flames for giving the four Sun Gods a fake name. "And if you call me 'pet' again, I'll castrate you then shove your balls up your arse."

I'm nobody's fucking pet.

"Lie." Dawn deadpans.

What the? I give him my evil death stare, but he just grins back at me. Guess Dawn knows when I'm lying. I steal a glimpse at Day, whose frown has somehow managed to deepen. If he's not careful he's going to get wrinkles on his immortal face.

Night pinches my chin, forcing my gaze back on him. "Name, and the right one this time."

I chew the inside of my lip as I try to think of a way out of this, coming up blank. "Dell." They can have the abbreviated version, hopefully they can't voodoo me with it, and at least I'm preserving *some* of my deteriorating dignity.

Night flicks Dawn a look, who nods at him before Night shifts his gaze back to me. He doesn't look all that sinister right now …

I remind myself he's a predator, if the stories are true. Not some chew toy for my inner bitch to gnaw on.

"Dell, who did this to you?" He motions towards my body in general, because apparently the whole thing's a wreck.

I'm not surprised, I don't need to peek under the thick folds of skirt to see the damage I know is everywhere. A lot is new, some is old, but I heal quicker than the others. No real idea why, it's always been a curse. Kroe was quick to notice and 'permission to beat' might as well be stamped on my motherfucking forehead.

I smooth my features, straighten my clothes, lift my chin and look him square in the eye. "Everybody."

Because it's true.

The countless lashes that mottle the skin on my back are from the women I stood up for, the ones who never repaid the favour. The bruises are from the beatings I took from my owner, for taking too long with a client or not long enough, for pleasing them too much or too little. Never on my face though—he likes to keep our faces pristine.

Or perhaps they're talking about the evidence of today's attack? That's simply a product of my life, a life I was prepped for since Kroe found me walking the streets, alone, when I was four years old.

My scars, the ones that really matter, aren't visible on the outside.

They frown, as if my answer displeases them. I don't care. I have nothing to prove to these men, nothing I want from them. I certainly have no interest in becoming their pet. Shut your labia, vagina. Nobody asked you.

Night continues to study me at close range, as if I'm interesting, even though I'm equivalent to a piece of shit on his shoe. An interesting piece of shit, apparently. He lets out a deep breath, glancing over my shoulder at Dusk behind me, before turning back to face Dawn and Day. "I get her first."

"Nobody fucking gets me! Psychos!" Because I have a death wish, though they all ignore me like the shoe shit I am.

Dusk growls like a dog and Day's hiss slices the air.

I flinch. They're intimidating, definitely control freaks. I need to steer clear, and put a chastity belt on my wayward vagina while I'm at it, because she likes a bit of bullying and I wouldn't put it past her to lead herself straight onto their abusive godly cocks.

"That's not how this works, Kal." Day moves forward so swiftly that his body's a blur, and now he's standing chest to chest with Night, whose name is apparently Kal. Hmm. Honestly wouldn't have picked him for a Kal. I would have thought him more a Lorenzo, or a Dario. Perhaps even a Raphael. Strange. Now I'm looking at him funny.

Kal doesn't cower, even though Day's taller than him. "Don't test me on this, Sol, you're not what she needs right now."

Sol? That's not a name I'd have picked for Day, either. Sol is too soft, makes him sound friendly. I think I'll just call him Day—at least that way I can continue to picture him as a sadistic, soul-eating prick with anger issues. What were their parents thinking? Oh, right … the sun made them. That explains it.

"And what do you think she needs, Kal?" Day challenges his darker equal.

"To be set free into the wilds with a handful of gold and enough food to feed a small army?" I say, though they fucking ignore me again.

If I wished for all that, would it take up all my three remaining wishes? I do a quick mental calculation. Yup. Then they'd follow me around until I 'repaid them', whatever that means, and I'd be shit out of ammunition. Ugh.

"Rest. Rehabilitation. Something all three of you suck at. At least with me she can heal."

Well, knock me over with a feather. Where did *that* come from? Kal isn't sounding so bad now …

"So, you're saying you don't intend to add her to your harem and fuck her into oblivion?" Dusk asks with a quirked brow.

Ignoring my vagina, who's relishing the prospect of

having her own cheer squad, I eye the back of Kal's head, willing him not to let me down.

He shrugs, the movement smooth yet heavy, because there's a lot of shoulder to shrug. "I'm not saying the thought hasn't crossed my mind. She looks like she needs a bit of enjoyment..."

Aaaand, there we go. Fucker. I had high hopes for Kal, too.

I step back into Dusks chest, who's controlling and likes to fuck's a lot. Shit, yeah, I really can't trust any of them. I shuffle forward again, exasperated with this inner tug of war I'm experiencing. If only they'd all just piss off. Although, then I'd be stuck in this strange, bright, colourful little world I'm in.

"How do I get home?" I ask, though, you guessed it, I'm fucking ignored again.

"I think you frightened her." Dawn—Captain Obvious over there. It must be written all over my face. Makes sense, I feel like I'm going to hurl my meagre guts up.

Kal looks over his shoulder at me and frowns, before turning back to face the other two. "You know I wouldn't do that unless she agreed to it, for fuck's sake." He sounds offended.

Day's stare cuts to me and my vagina does a curtsy. Behave, bitch.

Yup, he's still frowning. His poor skin, working so hard to hold up his immortal expectations despite the harsh conditions it's faced with. "Perhaps you are what she needs right now." He shifts his attention back to Kal. "But if she goes with you to the Kingdom of the Night then we're all coming with you. We stupidly invested in her too, so we all have the authority to make sure she doesn't throw herself off another cliff and land us all with a loss that none of us can afford right now."

Hmm, I wonder what that means?

"Don't I get a say in this?" I ask.

"No," they answer in unison.

I roll my eyes and mutter something about dominant Fae bastards, even though they all finally answered me, before Night wraps his hand around my arm and I'm whisked off in a wave of white fucking light again.

This is getting real old, real quick.

CHAPTER FOUR

We land amongst a sea of women—surprise, surprise. My vagina may be excited about meeting her cheer squad, but I'm fucking not.

The first thing I notice is they're all *stunning*. Of course. All draped with sheer material in a fashion that shows a lot of flesh ... nipples standing to attention left, right and centre. No uncomfortable corsets for them, pushing their breasts through the roof. And from what I can see, no scars. No missing limbs. No haunted eyes.

"I don't fit in here," I mumble, side-stepping a jumble of porcelain limbs and trying to ignore the moaning.

My sensitive nostrils itch from the thick scent of arousal, and I sneeze nose jizz all over my palm. Lovely. I surreptitiously wipe it on my skirt and hope nobody notices. Highly likely given the plethora of juices spurting here, there and everywhere.

The marble hall is furnished with day beds and plush lounging pillows—surfaces galore for draping bodies along and fucking them senseless.

Making our way towards the exit, we pass two women

pleasuring each other on a day bed, and a cluster of female limbs doing some tantric shit on the pile of pillows on the floor.

They look like they're having a great time, going by the sounds and the looks on their faces. I can't speak for their vaginas, though, that would be presumptuous of me. All I know is mine's got a mind of her own. Down girl!

Some women are even smiling, and not losing an eye for it. Not that it makes me feel any better about being lassoed into a fucking harem. I'm no prude, don't get me wrong, I'm just done with being owned.

A few of the ladies swarm Kal, tripping over each other in the process and looking far too eager to be boned by the God of fucking Night. I shuffle backwards to avoid being knocked out by a wayward boob.

Kal flicks a hand as if he's batting away a fly. "Not today, girls."

They pout. Like, actual pouting. It looks ridiculous on grown women. I never realised until now.

"Pfft." I can't help myself, though I instantly regret it when one of the girls gives me a disdainful stare. I remind myself that this is their normal, and I'd better not outcast myself because I'm probably expected to spend a lot of time with these women, and not all of it chatting about the weather. The last thing I need is a pissed off courtesan sinking her canines into my clit. If the shrinking of my labia is anything to go by, my vagina agrees.

Kal's leading our group through the sea of slippery vaginas, his shoulders tense, stride heavy.

"Were not staying here, then?" I ask, stepping over something that looks suspiciously like a castrated, petrified penis. I bet the girls have fun with that. My vagina's practically reaching down and grabbing it all on her own. She needs to learn to keep her labia to herself.

"No," says Kal, not looking back at me.

I roll my eyes and give a sad little wave to the penis toy. I'm sure it could fit in my pocket ... who needs a real one when you can have a fake one which does what you fucking ask it to?

"You're not exactly a friendly host. Do you treat all your guests this way?"

We close the doors on the orgasm party, entering a large courtyard caped in the night sky. I sigh. This is what I needed. Cool air and the cover of darkness, somewhere to fade into oblivion. Visually, at least. Maybe this isn't so bad after all ...

I don't realise I've stopped until someone picks me up, and this time, I don't fight. Because hell, I'm sleepy. Like, wow, incredibly fucking sleepy. I don't think I can keep my eyes open.

I mumble something incoherent and, despite myself, nuzzle into him, stroking the glitzy god wear like I'm petting a puppy.

"Three, two, one ..." Kal's voice. So, it's Kal holding me ...

Lights out.

CHAPTER FIVE

I wake feeling rested, wrapped in smooth sheets and nestled on a bed of clouds ... or what I imagine a bed of clouds would feel like. I run my hands along the smooth material and almost spontaneously orgasm. So fucking soft.

Damn, I feel good. I think I could take on the world right now. Except I'm a courtesan, trapped in an endless cycle of commissioned sexual favours.

Groaning, I roll over, stuffing my face into this heavenly pillow I have somehow acquired, and wonder where and how I managed to fall asleep on the job ... a goddamn plush job at that! And why the hell haven't I been skinned alive for it? This pillow smells like jasmine and verbena. One breath, two breaths ... FUCK.

Realisation hits me like a twelve-inch schlong to the face. I toss the hair from my eyes only to be assaulted by the sight of Kal, shirtless and splayed out on a black velvet couch near my excessively large fuck-ten-people-at-once bed with his hands behind his head, watching me.

"What the shit?" It's the first thing I come up with.

His bedroom eyes suggest he's been there for a while, watching me sleep like he's some sort of psychopath. "I'd like to ask you the same thing."

I glance down and see I'm dressed in a pair of shimmering, black pyjamas. Thank fuck I'm clothed. Though, how I ended up out of my skirt and corset remains unanswered. At least my tits and vagina are covered. From memory, having those parts out on display is a prerequisite for Kal's ladies, and I guess that's exactly what I am now. Sigh.

Out of the pot and into the harem.

My change of attire *also* suggests someone's seen me naked. I guess everyone's seen me naked ... stripped, whipped and banged, that's me. But the thought of someone undressing me while I'm lights out ... slowly, deliberately peering at the story of me ... that's different. Perhaps they magically whisked up an outfit change and didn't even get a peek in? Yeah ... I'll go with that.

Kneading my palms into my eyes, I feel the scrape of my scar across my right lid. I clamp my fist shut, drop my hands and return Kal's heavy glare.

"Don't try and hide it, I've already seen it. We all have."

Frowning, I glance down at my closed palm, then back up as he slowly rises from the couch, those spectacular abdominal muscles that could only belong to someone so otherworldly on show for my eyes only. I may or may not picture myself running my tongue over them, before reining in my wayward vagina. I swallow and try to focus on what's important here. They've all seen my scar, Kroe's mark on my palm ... they know what I am. Who I belong to. Maybe.

His eyes fade to black as he prowls towards me. He's hot as a smoking pipe but he's also frightening as fuck when he looks at me like that. Cutting, predatory, and it's making me want to hide under the covers like a hormonal teenager. I wish he'd just leave me alone with my vulva and the mental image of his abdominals.

I shuffle further along the bed, away from all that approaching manliness. "Where are the others?" I ask, trying to dissolve the tension.

He stops by the side of the bed, his eyes returning to their normal deep sapphire blue. "They left recently, had to tend to some business in their own kingdoms. I took you out of your induced sleep so I could speak to you in peace. I thought it would be easier for you."

Speak to me? Easier? Not fuck me five ways sideways? Strange. "Induced sleep? What's that supposed to mean?"

Before I can blink, he has my hand, his fingers prying my fist open. I try to tug away but he holds my elbow in place, rendering my arm useless.

"This isn't talking. I feel jibbed."

He traces his finger over the arc of my scar. Two circles, one within the other, the symbol of a courtesan—one without a uterus. One who's safe to fuck without protection. One who's 'owned'. It's practically a return label for rebellious whores who have a death wish. I'm going to be waist deep in cum if I'm sent back there. Maybe that's what they'll do with me once they lose interest in their pet mortal.

Fuck no, not going back there. I'd rather sling a cum shot.

"You're nervous … why?" Kal asks.

I shift, angling my body away from him as much as I can manage in my current checkmate. "I don't like being touched." Nosey fucker.

He draws a deep breath, gaze down. "You've been hurt a lot in your life." He looks at me, his expression is haunted. "I've never seen so much damage on a body before. None of us have … not on someone alive." He opens his mouth to say something else then closes it, shaking his head slightly.

"Spit it out," I snap.

They saw my body ... they fucking saw it all.

"Your scar ... your *other* scar?"

I snatch my arm away. "You had no right," I hiss. I want to hit something. Anything. This is too much ...

I climb out of bed and grasp a candlestick before I take my next breath. It's pretty, and probably irreplaceable, but I'm going to throw it. I'm going to throw it at his fucking head, knock him out cold, take a peek down his pants for curiosity sake, then pick that fancy as fuck chair up and fuck some more shit up rig—

Wow, how was I so *mad* a *second* ago?

I look down at the black, shiny candlestick. It has dangly glass things hanging off it that glimmer. I run my hand along the shaft, moaning a little.

So. Fucking. Pretty.

It jingles, and the jingles give me tingles. That make me want to mingle. With that man there, the God of fucking Night. In this fucking room. Ooooooh yeah.

"Take me. Take me all," I groan.

Was that desperate sounding? Of course not. I'm a fucking queen, and he shall have my clitoris.

God, he's smiling at me. But I can think of much better things to do with that mouth of his. His lips should become acquainted with my labia, I think they would get along swell.

I let my vagina lead me towards him. He's scratching his head with a sexy roguish smile plastered across those lips that have an appointment with my eager little beaver. Wink wink. Nudge nudge. Thrust thrust.

Wow ... he's sex on a stick. I'd like for him to stick his sex stick up my bu—

The door swings open and Dusk, Day and Dawn saunter in like they're on a mission from ground patrol.

"Getting into her head already, Kal? You know that's *my* department," Dawn drawls.

My head's *his* department? It belongs to neither of these fuckers. But I *do* want *Kal's* head between my legs, where it should rightly stay until my vagina's purring like a fat little overfed pussy cat.

"Couldn't fucking help yourself," Day the Soul Sucker growls.

I sniff at the air and get a good dose of male arousal, sending my sex juices barrelling for the exit.

Night stuffs his hands into the pockets of his black leather 'fuck-me' trousers, sighing deeply as he continues to watch me with a gleam in his eye that's making me want to fuck *him* fifty-two ways sideways.

He shrugs. "I couldn't help it, she was about to throttle me with a candlestick."

Candlestick? Oh, right, the one in my hand. I place it back on the side table, giving it another few thrusts down the shaft because I can't fucking help myself. The glass dangly thingies jingle dangerously. Oops. It's probably worth more than I could make in a lifetime, even with my A-grade vagina. Why was I angry again?

Dawn looks the most forthcoming. "What do you mean, getting into my mind?" I ask him, in my seductive bedroom voice that I hope makes Kal want to dance the maypole with me. I throw him a wink, just to drill it home.

Dawn smirks. "Kal can control your emotions. He can puppet your mortal brain."

Kal sighs and gives me a guilty smile.

The warm fuzzies I was feeling a second ago disappear entirely, and what *was* a vision of anal foreplay with Kal is now me picturing him in a choke hold. I shoot him a seething glare. He used fucking powers on me to temper my anger?

Fuck this shit, I'm out of here.

I head for the door. But one second I'm storming like a

badass and the next I'm paused mid-step, unable to move, perched precariously on one foot.

Day steps in-front of me. "Where are you going?"

Thankfully I can still talk, though I'm not sure why my body isn't working, and I'm hoping like fuck I don't topple over. "What have you done to me?" The panic in my voice is evident, not that it seems to soften Day's solid glare.

"We need answers, little mortal, and you're not going anywhere until we have them. So, turn around, walk over to the couch, and sit the fuck down."

With no hesitation, I oblige. What the shit? It seems Sol can compel me, which means I'm fucked. Literally. My vagina does a little jive. Crazy bitch.

"I hate you guys." I drop onto the super comfortable couch. My arse is happy, but my head is furious.

"That much is obvious," Kal murmurs.

I avoid looking at him. Bastard compelled my brain, and Day compelled my body. They're both on my shit list.

"Do you know how long you slept for?"

I refuse to answer shit listed Sol. Anyway, how the fuck would I know? I've been asleep. Duh!

"Sixteen days," he states.

If I could move, I'd probably fall flat on my face. As it is, a rather unladylike sound comes out of my mouth as I contemplate the implications of that statement. "How the hell did I sleep for sixteen fucking days? That's over two weeks!" I've been gone from the establishment for over two weeks.

Sssshit.

Hopefully they think I'm dead because I might as well be if I ever land back there. Kroe will make sure of that.

"Sixteen days is how long it took your body to heal from the abuse—cracked bones and internal damage—even at an accelerated rate. Sixteen days is how long it took us to mull over how you acquired all those scars that run too deep for us to heal." Day shakes his head, white hair flitting in front of his eyes. "We made a deal with you, all of us, even though it should be impossible to make deals with us now. It doesn't make any sense. You're an enigma to us, and now you owe us an explanation."

Oh dear, my closet skeletons are jingling. I ignore the fuckers and let Day go on with his rant.

He grabs my shoulders, shaking me a little. "We need to know who we have entrusted with part of our magic. Part of *ourselves,* for fuck's sake."

Say what? Well... this is a tide turner. I'm pretty sure I can work this to my advantage.

I straighten my shoulders. Correction, *try* to. But I can't, because I'm compelled to sit like a fucking statue.

"Let me get this straight," I say, with all the sass I can muster. "You guys placed a part of yourselves into me when you each granted me the rights to a wish? Was that the warm rush of whatever I got when I met each of you on that cliff?"

Four nods. Interesting.

"And what, do I keep it?"

"No." Dawn laughs. "Of course not. But by granting your wish, then taking one from you as equal payment, we become stronger. It's how we grow in strength. Well, it used to be."

I try to nod, like I know what the fuck that's supposed to mean. "So, until I take a wish from you all ..."

"And until we take something from you in return as payment ..."

"You're all stuck with me?" My gaze shifts to each of them and one by one, they nod.

"It's only three wishes now," Dusk states, clenching his fists. "Because you used my wish to try and kill yourself."

Wow, that was a whole lot of accusation all balled into a

few small words. I roll my eyes, because that's all I can do right now. "You really need to get over that."

Dusk is suddenly all up in my face, canines bared and looking like he's about to skin me alive. If I wasn't frozen in place, I'd be running in the opposite direction. But ... there's a warmth blooming between my legs. I let out a strangled moan, because fuck me, that's why. Zero to one hundred in two point five seconds, that's a record! Am I about to have a self-induced orgasm without even touching myself? I fucking hope so.

A sly smile spreads across Dusk's face.

"What the hell?" I gasp, between laboured breaths.

All four of their nostrils flare, jaws grinding. I know that look, it's restraint. I know that because it's something I never fucking see, and it doesn't take a genius to work out why their interests are piqued. I'm aroused, and they're High Fae ... their senses are phenomenal. I'm surprised these sinister gods aren't taking whatever they want from me right now.

Just before I careen over the edge of that orgasmic precipice, the sensation disappears. Poof, just like that. I cry out, because I'm all hot and heady—sweating bullets because what would have been a mind-blowing orgasm was just torn away from me.

"You don't want to get on the wrong side of me. I can either make this pleasurable for you, or not." Dusk's breath is a warm brush against my face, which I still can't move—bastard, and the scent washing over me is intoxicating. Focus, Dell, you hate these men.

"Personally, I prefer to watch you writhe in pleasure." He pulls back a little, before pausing. "And the name's Drake. Use it."

I swear I flinch, despite the fact I can't move. Hmmm, I think I just got a taste of Drakes controlling nature, and I'm not entirely sure I hate it, if the resonating ache between my legs is anything to go by.

I look him in the eye. "I thought you were the most attractive, but you just lost that title, because that was cruel."

His eyes darken and I smile inwardly. Fucker owes me an orgasm. He's shit listed until I get it. But my victory is short lived.

"It's my wish next, mortal," Dusk says, smiling. "And you're all out with me. So, I'd watch what you say because we Sun Gods do not like to lose, and I have plenty of ways to get right back at the top of your erotic fantasy list."

"Fantasy list my arse," I snap, then clamp my mouth shut before I say something else that will dig a hole deep enough for me to fall in and be unable to crawl back out of. Though right now, that's sounding rather pleasing, because Drake has a look on his face that indicates he wants to bend me over his lap and spank me senseless.

He takes a step towards me and suddenly my body's free from its confines. I scamper off the couch, perching myself behind Kal. Why? Fuck knows. He's on my shit list, too. But he's also the only one who's said things to me like 'easier for you.' And he didn't dress me like a whore while I've slept in his bed for the past sixteen days, which is astounding given I've been dressed like a whore for most of my life.

Day and Dawn look perplexed by this decision and Drake grinds his teeth, but he doesn't chase me. Kal places a protective arm back around me and I flinch.

Fuck … I've never been looked after before, especially not by a *male*. I just wanted to use him as a god barrier. I'm suddenly feeling claustrophobic, and it dawns on me just how fucked up this situation is …

I'm in a bedroom, with the four High Fae Gods of the sun cycle. Three of them have abilities that can control the shit out of my body and mind, and the fourth, Dawn, probably has some other badass ability like making me grow extra vaginas so he and his brothers can fuck me senseless at the same time.

I've got three remaining wishes to their four, but I'm a smart girl. Reasonably. Perhaps I should wish them out of my life? I know how to live off the land on my own—I bet I could make a nice little life for myself ... once I find my way out of this place, that is. I heard about a rebellion camp in the Eastern Territories. Perhaps we're somewhere close ...

"We're not," Dawn states.

I glare at him. "What?"

"I wish for you never to *wish* me out of your life. I'm taking you to the Dawn Kingdom, mortal."

Warmth washes over me as I continue to stare into those amber eyes. "Did you just read my fucking mind?"

He nods. "You're mine for the time being. There will be no taking off with my magic." He looks around at the others. "You guys can take care of yourselves, but if I were you, I'd give her a chance to settle in with me. Give her the space she needs before she wishes the three of you away and I'm the only one left with access to the full magic boost."

Fuck. Clever god. And he can read my mind. Has he been reading it this entire time?

"Yes. You think I'm pretty."

I feel my cheeks heat, and I know it's not from any form of magic.

"And you're right, I'm a sadist, though the pain I provide is pleasurable, and you would love it. But I would never take you against your will. You're safe with me, Dell."

Well fuck, that was a mixed bag. Strangely, I believe him. He's all stability with a calm intensity in his eyes. Honest.

Dawn smiles. "You'll find, Dell, that we're all honest. We literally cannot lie."

I feel like I'm not going to have to speak at all while I'm at the Dawn Kingdom, which is just fine with me. I'm used to silence. Plus, I don't want to get too comfortable and forget my plans to make myself an accommodating little life in the East.

"What's your name?" I squeak. Smooth, Dell. My vagina's rolling her eyes.

"Aero."

"Aero. The pretty one. That suites. Finally, a name I fucking agree with."

He smiles.

"Don't get too comfortable, Dell. We have unfinished business." Kal turns and strides out of the room, slamming the door behind him.

Well, fuck me. Somehow, I've pissed Kal off. Or perhaps Aero has. Kal was probably intending on keeping me here locked up in his little sex room until I gave in to his seductive ways. Whoops.

I may sound like a whore, work as a whore, and my vagina may fancy herself as a whore, but the truth is the opposite. I think. Hard to know really—I've barely had time without a penis prodding me to work out who or what I actually am.

"You'll be seeing me," says Day. "Don't get comfortable with Dawn." He vanishes in a flash of blinding white light.

Oooh, scary voice. I'm happy to part with him for the foreseeable future, though my vagina's pouting.

That leaves Dawn and Dusk. Aero and Drake. Two sides to the same coin.

"That was a dog act," Drake sneers.

"You're not privy to her delightful inner monologue," Aero drawls. "She was about to wish away all our privileges and take off with our magic. I did us a favour."

Drake laughs. "You did *you* a favour. Sure there was no other way around it. Fucker. You'll be seeing me at Dawn."

He turns his attention to me. "You owe me, Dell." And he's gone. Whisked off in a sea of blinding white light.

Lightheaded, I grab onto the obsidian pole of the four-poster, fuck-ten-people-at-once bed to steady myself. Even without the magic, I still find it appealing.

"So, I'm not on your shit list?"

Fuck ... that's Aero. I almost forgot he was here.

"Well that's not very nice," he says, sounding indignant.

I walk to the large bay window, peering through the glass and hoping to catch a glimpse of our surroundings, but all I can see outside is *black*. I look over my shoulder at Aero, who seems out of place in this excessive room furnished with heavy, dark pieces, black crystal accents and velvet soft furnishings. It was obviously designed specifically for Kal and all his nightly splendour.

"No. You aren't on my shit list." I plonk down on the window seat. "You can read minds, that's not something you can help. The others willingly used their shit on me. So, they got shit listed."

He quirks a brow and strides towards me. "Any suggestions on how to keep out of the shit zone?"

"Stay pretty." He smiles. "And don't crowd me. I get claustrophobic. I sleep on the roof at the ... where I live. When I can, anyway."

He frowns and I feel like slapping him, because I hate people feeling sorry for me. I resist. I am a lady, after all. That, and I'm pretty sure he likes pain, so he'd probably get off on it.

"I would." He looks straight at me, pupils thickening. "And you're not going back there. I'll find you lodgings that are a suitable alternative."

I nod, feeling overwhelmed. He's been reading my thoughts this whole time. Poor guy. Thankfully, I think they've been somewhat tame ... I must make a point to watch them from now on though—not so easy when you have a mental vomit disorder.

He wraps a hand around one of the bed poles. "I can't pick and choose what I hear, mortal. Unless I have a hand on you, I can only take what you put out. Like I said, that delightful inner monologue of yours."

Phew, what a fucking relief.

"And I can only *see* those thoughts when I touch you, but that process is uncomfortable. For you. It's very invasive and not something I do unless I must. So, no, I don't know much, which is frustrating for us all. And I couldn't access your dreams while you were under Kal's mental control."

One up side to being put to sleep for two weeks like Snow fucking White, because some of my dreams are a bit out there. Not gonna lie.

"Wait, so you were trying to listen into my dreams while I was asleep?"

He nods, stepping closer to me, eyes tracing my wayward locks then back to my face. "I tried. We weren't sure what we were dealing with, still aren't, and we needed some traction."

"You couldn't just get Kal to wake me from my fucking coma?"

He shakes his head. "You needed the rest. Your body was broken, and obviously your mind needed the break too."

That's just a nice way of saying I'm a crazy bitch.

Okay, so he heard that and he's frowning at me. A-fucking-gain. "Stop frowning! It makes me feel uncomfortable. And no, I'm not forthcoming. I've essentially been on my own since I was four, so I've never had someone to rely on, and I have no concept of trust. That's not saying I'm untrustworthy, I think I'm very trustworthy." I nod, to emphasise my point. "I've just never trusted anyone else. Why the fuck would I when everyone has a goddamn agenda?" I'm rambling. Great. I do that when I'm nervous. Sharing personal shit makes me nervous.

He smiles. "I enjoy your rambling."

I roll my eyes … again. I can't help it around these bastards.

He lets out a huff of breath, pursing his lips. "If you roll your eyes at me once more, I'll find a way to punish you. And believe me, you will like it."

Well, fuck me. That was hot.

"Only when you beg for it, mortal."

He reaches forward but I hold up a hand, halting his progress. "If you do that 'white light' thing again, I may actually consider roasting your balls for breakfast. Can't you just fly us there with your man wings? Where are they, anyway?" I take a peek behind his back. "Come out, come out, wherever you are, pretty Aero wings!"

I frown when nothing happens. They can't play hide and go seek forever…

He throws me a shit eating smirk before he snatches my arm and we're whisked off in a flash of, you guessed it, white fucking light.

Bastard. Maybe he has really small wings, and he's embarrassed about their tiny little feathers.

CHAPTER SIX

Thousands of cylindrical towers, one of which we're perched on top of, rise to varying heights from the glistening turquoise ocean surrounding the city. Made from some kind of shimmering rock, the towers glow in an array of delicate colours; every shade of rose, peach, and pink imaginable. Between the towers are arched bridges hewn from the same materials.

The palace rules from the centre of the city. Rising higher than any other structure, it's made up of many towers, architecturally joined and bathed in its own glowing aura. The city looks like a fucking sunrise, the palace its sun.

I've heard stories about the Dawn Kingdom, as I have the other High Kingdoms, but they can only be accessed if you have wings. Which I don't, because I'm not High Fae. Just your common Lesser Fae with no wings and therefore, no immortality. Yawn. Some super cute, delicately tipped ears, yes, and a certain lithe beauty that's always garnered me the wrong sort of attention, but no wings.

Nope, I'm super normal, y'all.

Though I'm yet to see any of the marvellous fucking Sun Gods sprout *their* wings. For all I know they might be teensy.

But this place is *teeming* with High Fae, both men and women, all flying around doing their thing. Whatever that is. Wait, did I say women? Strange ... now I'm seeing things? Lovely. Seems I've hitched a first-class ticket on the crazy boat, after all.

A man floats past us with a smile on his face, nodding to Aero in an obvious sign of respect before he propels himself past, grey wings pumping at the air and looking positively phenomenal at such close range.

The last time I saw a pair of High Fae wings so close was when King Sterling visited the precinct, to show his power and maintain law and order over us pitiful females. One of his guards came into our establishment, parading his wings about. They were spectacular—the feathers deep red with glistening black undertones to match his fiery hair.

I stared in awe. We all did. But then he picked me, bound me so tightly that my wrists bled while he fucked me in every orifice available until I finally passed out, which he beat me for when I came to. When he'd finished, he inserted one of his feathers deep inside me. Something to remember him by. Fucker. Once the High Fae guard was done Kroe wreaked his fury on me too, humiliated that I'd 'slept' on the job ... and with a High Fae! In other words, don't fuck up again, Cupcake.

I kept that feather as a reminder to never trust a High Fae. Or a male.

The arms around me clamp tighter as Aero inches towards the sheer drop at the edge of the building. I'm excited about the fall, can feel my heart pounding like a ...

We fall. I think I'm screaming but I'm not. I'm *laughing* as the sea rushes to meet us. When we're barely metres from the surface, Aero's motherfucking wings manifest, and I swear to god my vagina rubs her eyes in astonishment, because they are *massive*.

They scoop at the air, pushing us out across the water, so low I can smell the salty tang. We swoop in an arc and the city rises before us, then we're in it, twisting and turning around and between the glistening, granite towers.

But his wings! I can't stop looking at them as my curls whip at my face. The same colour as his hair, they ply the air with the sunlight catching them, blending and shifting the rich auburn tones into hues of rose, orange, yellow, and even pink. I love them. I want to touch them. Maybe even give them a little sniff while he's sleeping.

We glide towards a spacious, rose coloured balcony, one of many adorning the ample towers, and we land with a gentle thump. I reach out to touch the feathers as those glorious wings come to rest in front of us, encompassing us.

"Don't. It's not a good idea to touch my wings right now," he growls.

I tug my hand back, pouting. Where's the calm Sun God of ten minutes ago? Squirming from his arms, I spin to face him, but he turns from me, his wings puckering behind his back. He perches on the edge of the balcony, face turned away.

"I have business to attend. This tower is yours, use it however you see fit. Gail's inside, she'll be your attendee while you're here. Don't be afraid to ask of her whatever you desire." He pauses before continuing. "Don't jump off the balcony. You'll survive the drop but not the serpents that dwell in the surrounding waters."

And then he's gone, throwing himself off the side of the tower and into the nether regions. I'm stumbling towards the edge before I can catch myself, because I really *do* want to touch those fucking wings, but heed his warning, halting just shy of the fall. I imagine he's right ... death by mysterious sea serpent monster would not be a nice way to go.

I'm blasted with a rush of air as he swoops past, the tip of his wing coming to within inches of my face. I reel back, away from the edge, landing with a thump on my arse, no doubt his intention. I stare, mesmerised by the sheer size of his wings, the power as they pump, feathers rippling in the wind, taking him across the sea. I watch until he's nothing but a dot in the distance.

Moody High Fae God. Anyway ... nothing teensy about those wings.

Turning, I take in the beautiful craftsmanship, noticing the intricate swirls and patterns carved into the surface of the entire building. Somebody's probably spent decades decorating it, maybe longer.

I walk inside, through the doorway three times my height, and stop, gazing in awe at the lavish furnishings. Everything is crafted from the same rose-coloured rock the tower is built from, the soft furnishings all lush and white.

Looks uncomfortable. Especially that day bed over there ... all that shiny rock. Wrong! I stretch out like a fucking queen, even though we don't have a queen, but that's not my point. I'm totally channelling my inner queen right now. I close my eyes, content to stay right the fuck here, on this daybed, for the rest of my life.

"Ahem."

I jolt upright. A woman stands before me, her orange hair arranged in a bun, tailored white dress accentuating her curves. No sign of any wings, though she must have them to live in the Dawn Kingdom. I'm not surprised they're tucked away—they'd be a pain in the arse indoors, knocking expensive shit over and such.

"Sorry ... it's been a big ... couple of weeks, I guess."

"Yes." She smiles, studying me with eyes the colour of

honey. I wonder how much she knows. "I'm Gail. I'm here to help you with anything you need. Milord had several requests for your comfort, one being that you receive little interruption. So, I'll show you about then make myself scarce. There's a bell on the wall of each room you can tug whenever you need me."

"Ok." I nod, overwhelmed, a feeling which only increases when Gail shows me around my new Dawn 'home'. I have my own level for every goddamn room! My area stops halfway down the tower, which is apparently where Gail hangs out, prepares food and what not. Probably entertains nobles with her sexy melodic voice, before they feed on her pristine, High Fae vagina.

The ceiling to each room is high, like, three stories high, and a staircase spirals up the centre of the entire tower. I'm going to be so fucking fit. I'm guessing the winged ones use the vast balconies to get around, flapping about the place from one level to the next. Minus wings and eyeing the colossal staircase, I decide on one main level to settle myself into.

The bedroom has a small table for dining and a bathroom chamber too—everything I need. It's the highest, so it has a solid roof, which I compensate for by opening every door and window in the tower, despite the chill. I hate enclosed spaces. Gail doesn't question my strange actions, instead quietly helping me with the task before excusing herself politely.

Even with the windows open, however, I'm drawn to the balcony. I sit on it for hours, admiring the view, legs swinging over the edge until the sun begins to set ... and I've never seen anything so beautiful. The kaleidoscope of colours match the city's scape so perfectly, blending with and highlighting the buildings surrounding the palace as the sun gently sinks below the horizon.

If this is dusk, then dawn must be *spectacular* in this kingdom. A tear rolls down my cheek and I swipe it away. Where the fuck did that come from? I never cry.

Eventually the sun disappears and the air becomes cool. I peel myself off the ledge and wander inside, eyeing the enormous four-poster bed. Frowning, I give the mattress a push. It feels like you'd imagine it would, all puffy and soft and warm and … Fuck that. I don't deserve to sleep on top of a cloud when the girls at home are sleeping with dirty old men between their legs, or on a bed shared with seven other whores and nothing more than a filthy, torn blanket to keep them warm and a single pillow to share between them all.

No. Fucking. Way.

And I'm not ringing that shitty golden bell on the wall to call upon my 'woman servant', even though my stomach's rumbling loud enough to wake a sleeping schlong.

It doesn't feel right. None of it feels right.

I drag a small rug onto the balcony, away from the edge, because I'm smart like that, and curl up on top of it. I shiver, missing the warmth of the girls along my spine and front. It's a sisterhood that I can't explain, a belonging to someone, something. And though this place is fancy as fuck, it isn't home. Not without my girls.

There's something about the depth of the night that brings out the monsters. The worry monster, the guilt monster, the fucking homesick monster. I clench my fists and curl harder into myself, try to tell myself they'll be gone in the morning.

Problem is, *my* monsters really do exist, and I have a sinking feeling in the pit of my gut that I'll never truly escape them.

CHAPTER SEVEN

*H*ave you ever woken in the middle of the night and had no idea where you are? Yeah, it sucks. Even worse when you also have a big feathery man god hovering over you with a scowl on his face.

"Really? You *fell asleep* on the balcony?" Aero hisses, plucking me from the ground and placing me on my feet.

Oh, right. Dawn kingdom. Sexy High Fae God who left me here in a tower in the middle of the fucking ocean then took off in a huff. Winning at life.

"I couldn't sleep." Technically not a lie, considering it took me a while to actually get to sleep. It then occurs to me that Aero can read my thoughts, and he's now looking at me like I'm lying, which I kind of am. I roll my eyes, then catch myself as his eyes widen, and I remember his threat to douse me in pleasure filled pain if I rolled my eyes one more time.

"I'm keeping a tally, Dell, for when you're ready. And you already owe me one. By all means though, keep it up."

Yikes. I shuffle back a step, much to my vaginas dismay. I may seem all sexually astute, but my sexual maturity lies entirely around being a courtesan, not a normal fucking person with normal fucking feelings having normal fucking sex. I'm not sure that's even a thing. And if it is a thing, I'm not sure I'd get off on normal fucking sex. What even is normal? Would I know it if it slapped me in the face with a slippery cock? Except it probably wouldn't be a slap … more of a slide or a gentle prod. And what would I do with it then? What would I actually do with sex if I was offered it rather than forced the fuck into it?

Aero clears his throat. "Dell, please, rein your thoughts in, for the love of dawn."

I feel my cheeks heat. "Sorry." Fucking mind vomit.

He places a hand on the small of my back and steers me inside, now lit with hanging Fae lights. Pretty.

"Did you even try it?" Eyebrows raised, he motions towards the bed, still meticulously made.

"I like to sleep under the stars." Not a lie.

He shakes his head and sighs. "I'd like you to get changed, then I want you to come with me. I have something I need your help with."

I notice his brown leather pants are speckled with something dark, as is the cream tunic he's wearing. It's undone down the front and there are beads of something on his chest. I swipe my finger along one, smearing the ruby substance across his smooth honey skin and the pad of my finger.

Blood. Fuck.

"What the hell, Aero?" I take a step back and study him anew.

He struts past me, towards the dresser perched against one of the walls. Opening a drawer, he tugs out brown leather pants and a linen top to match his own attire. He hands them to me. "Get dressed. I'll wait on the balcony."

Snappy Aero. This is new. Not sure I want to go anywhere with *snappy* Aero. "Where the fuck are we going?"

"I'm not in the mood for questions, Dell. Just get dressed. Or stay here and miss out. Your choice." He storms outside.

This man.

After considering for a second, weighing my chances that I'm about to be either raped or slaughtered, and convincing myself it's unlikely, I jump into action. I better not be fucking wrong, then die for being nosey.

Once dressed I walk outside into the brisk air. Aero's standing with his back to me, but the moment I step onto the balcony, he spins around, throws his wings out, wraps me in his arms and hurtles himself backwards.

I gasp as the rush of cool air hits my lungs, but we don't fall far before he spreads his wings and we dip steadily towards the water. It crosses my mind that he's about to throw me to those mysterious fucking sea serpents, but instead we align onto a balcony almost at sea level, at the base of one of the palace towers. He puts me down and I stumble back a few steps, towards the slashing ocean ... away from the gloomy entrance.

"Where are we?" I sniff the air, my every sense on high alert. The stench of death surrounds me.

"The dungeon," Aero states as an orb before us is ignited to illuminate a small portion of the cavern.

"What the fuck are we doing in the dungeon?" Does he want to lock me up? Or is this part of a deviant sexual role play plan he has?

"No. And best not to put ideas in my head, mortal. It's fucked up enough already." He leads the way down a winding staircase that's scarcely illuminated.

"Duly noted." I follow him, because the mouth of this cavern is so close to the water that I'm not convinced one of said sea serpents can't reach in and snap up an unsuspecting Lesser Fae female.

We descend the stairs for what feels like hours, finally

arriving at another large cavern, illuminated by more glowing orbs. There are tunnels at regular intervals along the outside wall, branching off. It's down one of those tunnels that Aero leads me. We walk past numerous closed iron doors on either side which are faintly lit by smaller orbs.

"How much farther?" I ask. My emotions are starting to overwhelm me ... I fucking hate cells. Or small enclosed spaces. I may be used to them, but that's not by choice.

"Not far." He reaches back to take my hand, which I surprise myself by taking—my small pale one getting lost in his grasp.

"Seriously though, you're not going to lock me up down here, right?"

"I would never lock you up, mortal. You're safe with me."

If only that were true. I'm not safe with anyone, not even myself.

A few minutes later we come to a door at the end of the tunnel, which Aero produces a small, rusty key for. Hmm ... I watch him wiggle it into the hole.

Small tool. Disappointing.

He clears his throat as the door creaks and groans. Aero pushes it open to reveal ... not fucking much. It's too dark to see anything. But I can hear muffled breathing, from more than one person. He tugs me forward a few steps. The ground's smooth beneath my feet, slick with something ...

The room comes to light, illuminated by orbs dotted around the walls.

I gasp, then gag, my hand covering my mouth as I take in the scene before me.

Splayed and gagged along the wall, hanging from iron cuffs, are nine immortal High Fae guards. Their wings, spread behind them, are pinned with spears through the fine bones and into the stone wall they hang from. Their feet are cuffed at the ground, the blood running from their extensive wounds oozing onto the floor, pooling at my feet.

"What the fuck?" I leap to a spot that's not drenched in blood as I continue to take in the horror of the splayed Fae, who take up several metres of wall space each. Their wings are red tipped with black, and their hair, also red … just like the High Fae who left the feather in my cunt.

Something dark, savage and gritty awakens inside me. A beast, feral and unreasonable.

I'm frightened, because although she's only cracked one eye open, she's poised to pounce.

She wants revenge.

I'm not sure I could stomach what she has in mind.

I try to ignore it, avoid looking at their faces because I know if I see *his* face, the other eye will crack open. And then … I don't know what. Maybe I'll lose myself entirely. What little I have left.

I let out a strangled sob. "Why have you done this?"

"Your descriptive inner monologue, mortal. Which one was it?"

No. Fucking. Way.

I glare at Aero, whose eyes are entirely black, a sign he's royally pissed. His hair has fallen over one side of his brow, almost masking his left eye, making him appear cruel. I'm not convinced he isn't.

"He paid for my services you psycho!" An eye for an eye makes everyone blind, and likely *eight* of these men are innocent.

Aero takes a step towards me, holding out a large, serrated knife which materialised out of fucking nowhere. The kind of knife used for sawing wings from the backs of Fae. The sight of it makes my bones ache.

"It doesn't matter if he paid for your services or not. Tonight, he loses his wings."

Fucking hell.

Aero's not the calm one—I was entirely wrong about that.

"And you're wrong, Dell. None of them are innocent. When I asked them each if they took a small, Lesser Fae female with long white hair and scars on her back in non-immortal territory, then left a feather in her vagina, knowing who I am and what I can do, each of them internally confessed to deeds either much worse or *just* as bad. Worse, they *relished* in those thoughts." He takes another step towards me. "I could invade their head spaces, find out which one was the man who assaulted you, but I'd rather you point him out for me before I slice the wings from his back." He pushes the dagger in my direction. "Or, you can do it."

Woah. Fucking woah.

I take two steps back towards the open door, even though the beast inside me is purring.

"I'm not doing this. I'm not being part of this. If you want to be a savage that's on you, I have enough nightmares already without throwing *this* in the mix." I gesture towards the men before me, splayed and broken. "You don't know me at all if you—"

"*He raped you.*" Aero's voice is a rasp.

The beast crawls up on her haunches … I shake my head, forcing her down again, reining her in.

"He fucking paid for it, Aero! They all did!" I stare at him, aware that I'm trembling, aware that I'm so close to losing my goddamn mind because I can't save these cocksuckers from losing their wings. The beast inside doesn't discriminate between the varying shades of darkness—she wants nothing more than to castrate them *all,* before leaving them to bleed out on the filthy dungeon floor.

But she's not in control right now, I am.

I lift my hands to my head, close my eyes, breathe,

breathe. I open them again, looking at Aero, pleading, *willing* him to understand. "I'm a courtesan! Men pay to fuck me!"

"Not like that," he growls. "Never like that."

"But it *is* like that!"

Aero takes another step closer to me, bunched fists, white knuckles, wings spread wide. "Which one?"

My beast wants a go ... she wants a piece. She wants to tear through him then tear through those men over there, ripping them limb from limb.

Fuck.

"No. I'm not doing this," I whisper, because perhaps if I'm calm, he will be too. And her ...

"You don't have to." He's reaching forward with his hand, and I know what he's about to do. He's about to invade my personal space and draw the information from my memories. He's lost all sense of boundaries!

I scurry backwards, afraid of what he'll see. What he won't be able to un-see. "Don't, Aero. Please ... don't." I take another scrambling step backwards. My beast is cowering now. No, she's fucking gone altogether.

He pauses.

I need to go. I need to get away. I need to run.

I turn from the scene and flee ... running from the beast inside me, the one I'm not sure I can control. I run from myself, and I run from the screams of the splayed men as Aero saws their wings from their bodies, rendering them Lesser Fae ... rendering them mortal.

Just like me.

Reaching the cavern, I stumble up the stairs we came down earlier, gasping, fumbling, sometimes *clawing* my way, with only the meagre light of the Fae orbs to guide me. It's a brutal, punishing ascent that shreds meat off my elbows and knees, cutting through the leather covering my legs.

I make it to the cavern at the top, the one we first entered.

I run through the gloom, unsure of the direction I'm taking, my only guide the tang of fresh, salty air. I just want out. I want fucking out.

I sense it before I feel it, but it's too late ... I smash into something thick and slimy, heavy with the smell of rotting flesh. It wraps around me, catching me in a tight embrace. I feel like I'm being squeezed to death by a giant fucking schlong, and if I weren't about to die, I'd probably laugh at the irony.

Two yellow eyes stare at me through the darkness and a wash of warm, rancid breath assaults my senses. My eyes adjust and now I see the fucking teeth—and they are plentiful. A jagged smile that's partially open, threatening to snap me in half. Or chew me slowly, bit by bit. Either way ... I'm fucked. I can't move, can't even yell. And forget about breathing, my lungs are bound so tightly.

This thing looks like a giant eel, crossed with a snake, crossed with a penis, sans testicles, and it's frightening as shit. I'm about to die, and yes, it's going to be a shit way to go. Soon I'll be part of the carrion between his teeth that's making his breath smell so incredibly rank—like something dead crawled in there and died all over again.

Is that a blue feather between his teeth, attached to a piece of shattered bone and skin? I gag.

A long, forked tongue flicks out and dances across my face. It's rough, gritty, but it's not an assault. In fact, it's more like a caress. His grip on me loosens and I draw a deep, shuddering breath, but don't allow myself to hope. He's probably just savouring his meal.

Where's Aero? What's the point in having a fucking Sun God as an escort if he doesn't save me from a giant penis serpent?

"Because I can hear his thoughts. He's not going to eat you, Dell."

Fucking hell. This dick.

"Easy for you to say!" I whisper yell at the disobedient god over there, lurking in the shadows while I'm being wrung out by a fucking Fae eating penis serpent.

His tongue disappears and his teeth draw close. He tilts his head, coming eye to eye with me, and they're big, yellow and knowing. I swear to the psycho gods, there's a world of knowledge in those eyes.

Have you ever had a moment where you feel like you just *connect* with an animal? I'm having one now, with this giant penis serpent. Perhaps he doesn't want to eat me after all.

I wriggle my hand free, reach up and tentatively stroke his face, hoping like fuck he doesn't change his mind about what's on the menu tonight and chomp off my arm. He's smooth, slimy, and kind of gross, but I suck it up because I need to be brave.

Hang on ... he's leaning into my touch, and now he's ... rumbling? Wait, is he fucking *purring*?

"Yes," Aero states from not too far away, a surprised lilt to his voice. "That's exactly what he's doing."

A purring penis serpent. Wow, never thought I'd see the day.

I don't shift my gaze from him, because I'm transfixed. Also, I don't want to startle him and become dinner again.

Finally, he pulls his head away, his body unravels and he slithers backwards out of the opening in the side of the building, blinking at me once more before he disappears into the gloom with a splash.

"What the fuck was that all about?" My voice sounds calm, despite the stampede of blood surging through my veins, making me feel like I'm jacked up on something incredible. "I thought those things were lethal."

"They are," Aero says, his voice coming from right behind me.

I spin, still paranoid about him touching me and digging through my mind without my permission. But he has his hands held up in submission.

"I won't try again, not without your permission." He sounds cautious, as though he's concerned the penis serpent whisperer will throw herself off the ledge to be with her vast kingdom of penis serpents indefinitely.

I glance around, trying to find another way out of this dungeon. He's drenched in blood, it's even on his face and his scent is caped in it. There's no way in hell I'm letting him carry me when he looks like a mass fucking murderer ...

"You're covered in blood too, Dell ..."

Don't try to make this about me—fucker! Even so, I look down ... and he's right. But it's my blood, not *theirs.*

He whips his shirt off and I look away, because my vagina doesn't need to see that right now. He throws it on the ground, then jumps into the water before I can scream his own goddamn warning at him. He's going to get eaten by a penis serpent and I'm going to be stuck here forever, in this fucking dungeon. Great. Just fucking great.

But then he's clawing his way back onto the balcony, dripping wet and clean. "Was that all you were worried about? Getting left in the dungeon? I didn't hear an *ounce* of concern for my life."

That's because you're a fucking psycho.

"I heard that." He straightens and saunters towards me. I do my best to ignore everything from the chin down as he dries himself with his shirt then splays his arms wide. "Clean, see? No reason for me to not carry you now."

"It's the blood you can never wash off I'm wary of." I swat a lump of matted hair from my face.

"You can't expect me to be pure because I never have been, never will be. But I'm real and I'm honest and ... I'm not going to hurt you."

I step back, arms crossed.

"Dell ... please, you're freezing."

He's right, I am fucking freezing. In fact, my teeth are chattering and I'm pretty sure my internal organs are doing the same thing. Hmm, I don't want to *die* down here ...

I waver, pause, drop my hands. I can smell death and blood and I want out of this shit hole. I'm so fucking cold.

He closes the last few steps between us, wraps his arms around me, takes us to the edge of the balcony and spreads his wings. They glisten in the moonlight, appearing black, and I almost lose my stomach when, with two hard beats we're in the air and ascending rapidly towards my tower.

My tower. Full of lush things I can't bring myself to appreciate.

A savage chill bursts through my body, limbs trembling as my teeth clash together violently.

"Fuck," Aero says, pulling me close. "Hold on Dell."

CHAPTER EIGHT

We land with a thud on my bedroom balcony and Aero carries me swiftly to the hearth inside. It's deeply set with a semi-circle of steps leading down to the small sitting area before it. He sets me down on one of the massive pillows scattered around, pumps a fist and his hand glows as a blazing orange flame engulfs the wood stacked neatly in the centre of the hearth, creating a wash of instant heat. Which does fuck all because I'm chilled to the bone.

How did I get so goddamn cold?

"Adrenaline was pumping through your body, so you didn't realise. Shit …"

Aero tosses more wood on the fire before taking off, making a round of my room and shutting every door and window. He turns his attention back to me and my bloody clothing.

"N-n-n-no f-f-f-uckin-g-g w-w-way."

Too late, he shifts to my side and starts removing my clothes. I feebly try to push him away, but the parts of me that aren't numb hurt so bad I can't get anything to work.

He removes my tunic with deft, expert care, leaving my undergarment, for which I'm grateful. Next to go are my tattered pants, which he simply tears from my body like a sexual predator.

"Who's to say I'm not a sexual predator," he drawls. But I know it's a farce because there's an edge to his voice and an urgency with his movements that's not sexual *at all*. Which means I'm probably in a really bad way. In saying that, there would be worse ways to go than freezing to death—surely it would be like falling to sleep? Better than suffocating on a penis.

"Can you not, Dell. For fuck's sake."

Someone's channelling their inner fun sponge.

Next, he removes his own pants, and I can't help but admire …

He pulls me close, pressing the length of his body against mine. "You're going to be fine."

You know what Aero? Death is a natural part of life. I've had most of my existence to come to terms with that. Perhaps Dawn needs a lesson in mortality.

He breathes a huff into my hair that could be frustration. Maybe he's getting sick of me already? Good. Perhaps they won't want to keep me as a pet after all. He's lasted less than twelve hours, I wonder how quick I can flit through the other three and be free?

Fuck, I'm cold. And yeah, all that honey skin pressed all over me is making me ramble internally, seeing as my teeth are still clanking together and I can't speak. My vagina's quiet for once, probably because she's frozen solid. Strangely though, I'm not opposed to this touching thing, perhaps because I don't feel like this man wants to fuck me seven ways sideways right now …

"Dell!"

Oops, there he goes, growling again. I'm the one who should be angry! Guess I'll worry about that if I survive this hypothermic attack.

He wraps himself around me tighter and I let out a small choking sound. I'm pretty sure all this squeezing is preventing the blood from flowing back to my extremities.

"Sorry," he mumbles, loosening his hold on me. "Immortal strength."

I make a small sound through my nose, feeling myself start to drift as a blanket of warmth slowly envelopes me. I'm so comfortable now ... and so fucking tired.

"Don't go to sleep, Dell." His words are firm, commanding.

I can sleep if I want to sleep ...

He groans and ...

There's mum, my lovely mum. People shunned her, were afraid of her appearance—the skin on her face and bald head all melted and distorted, one eye fused permanently shut, the other a beautiful silver hue ... the same as mine. She never frightened me, and I run to her now. She's holding out her arms but just as I reach her, she fades.

"Don't go, Mum! Please ..."

There's a terrible pressure inside my head. I buckle beneath it, fighting against it as it tries to steer me towards a dark corner I don't want to see. I'm not going there, not right now. I can't.

My surroundings flicker. Light, dark, light, dark ...

Figures hover, talking. Something about herbs not working on me ...

I see blades—dirty, blunt.

Fuck. No! No! No!

I try to move, to get away.

I can't.

Rough hands hold me down, voices angry now.

Searing pain tears through my abdomen and I scream and scream and scream ...

I go into a daze where I'm beyond pain but eerily aware of everything that's happening to me.

Flies land on my face, my body, as my reproductive organs are scooped out of me with a giant spoon and placed in a bowl, checked over, then tossed in a bin with the rotting flesh from other victims who suffered the same treatment before me.

I vomit and start to choke, inhale it, trying to die. My head is pushed to the side and it spills to the floor.

Let me fucking die!

I see only blank faces, but I know who they are ... I have their identities stored.

I know who you are!

Something scrapes along my conscious and an image appears, but it's murky, distorted, because I'm battling something—a mighty force that's working its way into my mind. With it comes a sharp, agonising pain.

My inner beast peels her eye open, purring like the cat that got the alley rat. But she hasn't ... not yet. She's waiting for that image to clear. She crouches, low and eager, tail swishing—ready to pounce ...

The force slices into my mind again, bringing with it that searing pain. I scream, because it's fucking agony and I'm fighting against them both, the beast inside and this mental fucking blade.

The image becomes clearer ... no, no. NO!

I wake, gulping air, still wrapped in Aero's arms, his hand plastered around the side of my head.

Oh god, the pain ...

The image solidifies, clears, and I scream again, jolting

him awake. His eyes widen, turn from molten amber to jet-black in an instant.

I'm powerless, immobile ... tethered to his hand that's plastered to my head, clawing at my memories, searching for more. More. More. I plead with my eyes ... try to focus.

Let me go, motherfucker!

He looks confused, and now he's whipping his hand away and unwrapping himself from my body so fast you'd think I have a highly contagious disease. I gasp, hands shaking, and flop back on the pillow, reeling from the assault.

He's standing a distance away, trembling, fists clenched. "I'm sorry ... I was asleep, I didn't know I was doing it. I've never done it in my sleep before ..."

With all the other women he does this with? Lovely fucking image right there, thanks. Makes me feel special.

"Dell ..." He takes a step forward, but I raise a hand.

"Don't."

I feel violated, exposed. Even though he didn't mean to, he promised he wouldn't without my permission. He didn't get far, not far at all really ... perhaps it would've been different if he wasn't asleep. He still dug up some painful shit ...

I'm checking to see that my high waisted panties still cover my scar, which they do. Thankfully. That shits ugly. I hate looking at it, and I hate other people looking at it. Hard to avoid when you're a courtesan, but I have special pieces which give those literal fuckers access to all the important bits while keeping the scar covered. We all do.

Now he's growling like a beast, his eyes hooded and shadowed.

"Woah, calm the fuck down." I shuffle back along the pillows, because his wings are coming out and he looks positively menacing. Like he's ready to slit some throats and shed some blood, then probably fucking dance in it.

He's pacing along the front of the hearth with his wings puckered high on his back. They keep flexing then tugging in close again, like they want to fly on their own.

Why the fuck is *he* angry? I'm the one whose mind's been violated!

He moves so fast he's a blur, and he's suddenly on top of me, wings fanned out around us, making a small cave in which only the two of us exist. And my vagina of course. It's warm and smells like citrus and sage. Not my vagina, the space we're sharing. It would be strange to have a citrus and sage smelling vagina. I'm kind of forgetting just why I'm angry at him with all this sharing of breath that's going on.

"I didn't want to see it, but I fucking did, and now I can't un-see it, Dell." His breath feels hot on my face, his voice a low rumble. "Let me in again, please."

"Are you kidding me?"

His arms, bent at the elbows, tremble with the effort of holding himself above me. "I'm not kidding, mortal. Let me in."

I very nearly do, because, while this living man cave is intimidating as fuck, I can feel the press of his half naked body against mine ... I'm no saint. My vagina likes it rough, I know that much, and I know Aero would give it to me just the way she likes it. And now I'm picturing things and my pussy's throbbing, dampening. Fuck. I can't really blame my vagina for this one, I'm pretty sure my mind's doing half the dirty work.

A bulge is growing against my thigh. I suck in a gasp, my body automatically pressing closer to him ... screw you, body, you traitor. You've changed.

"Fuck." Aero growls, nostrils flaring as he undoubtably scents my unsanctioned desire. He pushes himself away from me and stalks up the stairs of the fire landing, heading straight to the balcony door. His wings are flared, all six or whatever the hell metres of them. He puckers them in to get through the door and then throws himself off the side and disappears into the deep of the night.

Fucking gone, just like that.

CHAPTER NINE

"What have you done to him?"

I'm jolted awake from where I fell asleep by the door, waiting for Aero to return like a desperate fucking housewife. Day's staring down at me, those glacial eyes positively sinister, like I'm some sort of criminal. Why does he look angry at me?

"Nothing!" I sit up, tugging the thick blanket around my neck. I managed to track down some white silk pyjamas in one of the drawers, but the air has a chill to it, like the sun has been gone just a little too long …

Oh fuck …

I clear my throat, school my features and peer up at him through my lashes. "It's not supposed to be night still, is it?"

"No, it isn't." Day's features sharpen as he continues to study me, but his answer is calculated and paced, like he's repressing his baser urges.

Yeah, I can spot that.

"While Kal's basking in the glory of having night drag on, the power should've shifted to me three hours ago. So, tell me … what did you do to Aero? Because he's never missed a fucking sunrise, not in all his very, very long existence."

Okay, so he's old. Like, great-great-great and then times it by fifteen grandpas old. Yeah, my vagina still wants to ride his god cock while he pounds her into oblivion, but only once I'm no longer angry at him, because my mind still has *some* fucking sense left, even if my vagina hasn't. Someone's got to be the sensible one.

I know! Then I'll head to the East and start my modest little life selling fruit, or something else mundane and boring as shit. Then I'll get old, wither away, and die—with all this knowledge that bears such a weight on me tucked away in my god-forsaken head, as I leave this world to their shit. Good plan.

I shrug. "I have no idea. He took off hours ago and hasn't returned. His eyes were all black and fucked up and his wings seemed to have a mind of their own."

Day kneels and takes my shoulders in his hands, his features softening. "What happened leading up to it, Dell?" His tone is sincere, probably because he wants information from me. I take note that he hasn't compelled me again, yet …

Perhaps someone hates being in the sin bin. Or, shit list bin. Awww, maybe he cares a little. Cute. Maybe I'll start calling him Sol after all. Fuck, not gonna lie, he's nice to look at. All that white hair and shoulders that would be good for hanging my knees over, and I *know* Sol would give it to me rough. The fact that he hasn't compelled me to fuck him yet, even though he has me entirely to himself right now, has scored him brownie points in my eyes.

Woah, fucking woah. Think I'm forgetting about the big issue here …

"Mortal?" Sol's nostrils flare, probably scenting my desire, sending my mind even deeper into the ditch where my vagina has built herself permanent lodgings. I shake my head. Concentrate, woman. Don't be lulled by her hormonal trickery.

"So ... he brought me men to slaughter, then I almost froze to death." I shiver at the thought. "Then we fell asleep practising some very PG skin to skin, and he tried to pry into my head while I was sleeping, which I didn't fucking appreciate. Then he lost his shit, went all freaky Fae on me, and left. End of story." I hiss a little because Sol's hands have tightened their grip on my shoulders, likely bruising the skin. My vagina's bowing down in submission because she loves the way he's grabbing at me.

Next thing, he's dropping his hands and yanking the blanket right the hell off me. He tosses it to the side and scans my body, which is fully clothed, I'd just like to reiterate.

His nostrils flare. "You're fucking hurt again, I can smell it."

I roll my eyes. What is it with these men and wounds? They seem offended by them, which is weird. Most men get off on them. "Yeah, I took on a set of stairs and lost. I'll heal." I glance down at the smudge of blood that's seeped through the white silk. Oops.

He pushes up the pants leg, exposing the wound on my shin and hissing, before swiftly tearing it all the way to mid-thigh. I almost slap the bastard, which would probably garner me a one-way ticket to the guillotine.

"What the fuck? Are you allergic to manners?"

He peers at me through thick lashes as he rips at my other pants leg and quirks a condescending smile. "I'm done pretending to be gentle."

Ahh ...

He stands, eyeing me all over, then huffs out a sigh. "Stand, walk inside to the tub, then wait at the edge for me to undress you further."

I choke on my own surprise, even as my traitorous body heeds the command from his fucking compulsion, and obeys. This is ridiculous, he's way too overpowered for one Sun God.

I'm all disappointed now. Guess this is what happens when you're led down the garden path by the fucking vagina. Idiot. She got my hopes up, even convinced me Sol was actually a good sort who deserved her juices.

I'm growling as I walk through my chambers, with Sol at my heels. No, not Sol. Day the Soul Sucker now and forever because he manipulated me into thinking he deserved my vagina, and now I really want to rip him a new arsehole as I stand at the edge of this ridiculously overstated bath, large enough to fit thirty compelled Dells—waiting for him to fucking undress me.

Fuck my life. How did I get here?

"Turn," he commands, and I turn to face him.

"Smile."

His mouth quirks a little as a smile tugs at my angry face. He nimbly works the tiny buttons of my top undone, probably because he's done this a trillion times, to a trillion different women.

Wow, that thought really dried up the dam.

"Why are you doing this?" I chime, through the biggest goddamn smile I've ever graced this world with. He pushes the silk top from my shoulders and watches it pool to the ground.

Next, he hooks his fingers through the waistband of my pants, the skin there clenching disloyally from his touch. He tugs them down, giving the material extra leverage as it catches on the round of my arse. "Step out of the pants."

I fucking obey, rolling my eyes as I do so. I bet that looks strange with a fake smile plastered on my face. This arsehole's at the top of my shit list for the rest of his immortal goddamn life.

I stand there in my chest wrap and high waisted panties, which display my arse perfectly, if I do say so myself. Not that he deserves such a sight right now. If I could move, I'd be smacking that smirk clean off his gorgeous face.

My shredded skin is on full display, looking very out of place in this massive, ornate bathing chamber that's all pristine and blushing pink. The wounds have started to scab a little, though most of them still look angry and red around the edges. Shit, I should've cleaned them before they started to heal, like Marion taught me.

He starts to unravel my chest wrap with sturdy, confident hands. I sigh through my stupid smile that's making my jaw ache, dropping myself into the mentally numb state I initiate whenever I'm about to be pounded by yet another unsanctioned penis ...

But yeah, that's about as far as *that* thought goes.

There's a sudden whoosh of air and a great deal of feral Fae hissing as Day's pinned against the wall by Aero, looking brutal, primal and ... I'm not going to lie, fucking hot.

Dressed in brown leather pants with nothing on his top half, his wings are spread wide, taking up a vast amount of space in the room I thought was rather spacious before. Now it seems small.

Do I break them up? Day looks calm as a fucking cucumber. Maybe he has this. I can't bloody move anyway so the point is moot. Actually ... why the fuck does he look so calm?

"You're smarter than that." Aero hisses at Day again, who's smiling like a psycho. That's weird ...

Oh ... I get it! Aero probably got some sort of telepathic godly 'ping' when Sol entered his Kingdom!

Bastard.

I whip my chest band back into place with the fierceness

of a wolf who just caught the scent of blood. At least Day's hold on my will seems to have been severed—speaking of which, I can't wait to cut his testicles off for using that shit on me again.

"You used me as bait!" I bellow at Day as I stride towards them.

Neither of them looks at me though ... too busy having an unspoken conversation between themselves as Aero keeps Sol pinned against that blushing pink wall like a rag doll. Though something tells me Day's letting Aero get the better of him ...

"You're good bait. He can hear your thoughts wherever you are." Day keeps his gaze pinned on Aero.

"Fuck off," I say, pausing a couple of metres from them, where I figure it's a safe distance to stand. Don't want to cop a feather to the eye and lose an eyeball. "What makes you think that?" Because that's suddenly more important to me than the fact that I just got used as Fae God bait. Good priorities are important.

Aero's muscles are bunching and shifting, like he's fighting against some unseen force.

Day shifts his gaze to me. "I *know* he can, because I can now feel your life force no matter how far I am from you. Now, be a good little mortal and get in the bath. Your scent is sending him rabid right now."

What the hell does he mean by that?

Aero peers over his shoulder at me, and it's enough to send me scampering back a few steps, because he looks fucking criminal. His features have darkened, sharpened, his canines have elongated, and the whites of his eyes are completely gone.

"What the devil ..." I step back and stumble on the edge of a rug.

Aero catches me before I hit the ground, his movement so

swift it was a blur. But he's rough, as if he doesn't know how to be gentle right now. I scramble out of his arms and dash behind a lounger that probably doubles as a sex prop. Aero crouches, watching me with hooded eyes. Maybe I'm prey right now, I'm not entirely sure...

"'Devil' is probably the appropriate terminology." Day straightens his tunic and pants that hug the bulge between his legs like a fucking candy wrapper.

Aero hisses.

Day lifts a brow, before returning his attention to me. "We're equal parts light and dark, Dell. We're the perfect balance ... most of the time. But somehow, you've managed to tip Dawn the reliable here, too far over the edge and now he's all instinct and predatory compulsion with zero goddamn sense." He gestures towards Aero.

There's something about Aero's feral leer, the darkness seeping from the man that was so bright earlier.

Yeah, I know...

I recognise it.

This ... this is his monster within.

"She's scared of you, Aero," Sol drawls, picking at an invisible piece of lint on his sleeve like he's bored fucking shitless.

Aero's nostrils flare and his gaze narrows. He stands, unfurling his body bit by glorious, frightening bit. Fuck...

I'm shaking. Whole body trembling because he literally seeps an aura of malice right now. I *know* he could likely fuck us all up with little more than a mere thought, taking the dawn with him. What would happen to the rest of the sun cycle then? And my vagina chooses *this* moment to think about what it would be like for him to be fucking her in this state.

His wings flare, feathers ruffling, chest heaving. He bunches his fists, breathing sharply through his teeth.

Oops, did I do that?

Day rolls his eyes.

Apparently my scent is sending Aero crazy; I think my *thoughts* might be doing the same.

This is my fault. Dawn hasn't initiated, and we're immersed in an endless night because of *me*. He came because he thought I was in trouble. He came because he thought Day was about to get physical with me, which it turns out he wasn't. But that's not the point. He came to save me even though he knew I'd be frightened of him this way; even though he didn't want me to see it. He came.

The thought gives me courage, even though my body's slow to catch up. I force myself to take a step forward, stepping around the sex lounger and towards my broken Dawn God. Then another. He's watching me like a hawk scanning his prey.

"Mortal," Day warns, and he's no longer calm. "He could break you right now …"

Yeah, I get that.

I steady my hands, except for the slight tremble I just can't still, and take another step towards the God of Dawn. Then another, and another.

"Whoever said a mortal pet was a good fucking idea," Day mutters.

Ouch, that stung. But hey, this was not my bright idea, fucker!

"Aero," I say, when I'm four steps away. "I need you back." I pause, because I'm not sure how close I should get. "I need you to come back to the light."

"You need me inside you, that's what you need." Aero takes a sudden step forward. I flinch but resist the temptation to fucking run.

Woah horsey.

I'm aware of Day's wings coming out. They're hard to miss when they're so fucking *big*. And silver.

Aero turns to face Day, hissing through his teeth. "Mine!"

Ahhh, say what?

Yeah, this whole situation needs to come to an end. I draw a deep breath to steady myself and take that last bridging step forward, placing myself in the centre of Aero's wide chest. He doesn't take his eyes from Day until I place both of my hands on his chest. His attention snaps down and his wings wrap around me, creating an Aero cocoon and washing his scent all over me. Peering up, I take his regal darkness right in, finding a comfortable place for it to sit inside me.

I need to give him something, something to take the edge off. To claw his way out he needs to dive back into the pit that set this off in the first place. I can't believe I'm even entertaining this idea. I'm definitely going crazy. Well … crazier.

"You can go back in, but please, only go where I allow you to …" I ignore the tremor in my voice, the banging of my heart against my chest wall, the taste of bile rising in my throat. I'm facing my worst fear right now.

He nods his recognition, and I hope, acceptance of my terms. His hands leave my waist and creep up to the sides of my face. I take a deep breath.

Sweet, sadistic Dawn God.

The pain hits me like a blunt force to the head. It's more painful than I remember, more invasive, probably because the bastards conscious and all dark and scary. I crunch my eyes shut. Whose great idea was this?

The pain subsides and my mother and I are in our small shack we call home. I've just woken and we're snuggling on her bed, *our* bed. She's running her hands through my curls and there's a smile blooming across her distorted face. She tickles me and I laugh, the sound like a chime of the sweetest bell.

I was happy once, Aero. See the smile on my face as my mother wraps me in a thick woven throw? Do you feel it? How happy my heart was?

She picks me up, cradling me in her arms. Her little blanket sausage. Then she throws me, and I bounce on the bed in a rolling fit of giggles, my hair fanning out across the sheets.

I'm happy, Aero.

Happy.

She's unwrapping me, and I'm so lost in the moment that I almost forget what's coming next ...

I need him out of my head. Right now ... because I'm about to come tumbling out of that fucking throw, and he can't see it.

The show's over. Aero let go.

Aero, let go *now*!

He releases me and I become slack in his arms, relief surging through me.

"Thank you," I croak. Why does my voice sound so brittle?

"Because you were screaming," Aero says.

I peer up at his face, and it's normal. Beautiful, bright, and pretty as fuck. He lifts me, holding me close to his chest as he walks us out of the bathing chamber and towards the balcony.

Is this when he throws me off the side and feeds me to the penis serpents? I wouldn't blame him ... I'm causing all sorts of issues right now.

"I'm not feeding you to the penis serpents, Dell."

We reach the edge of the balcony. Aero just used my derogatory term for sea serpents in general conversation. I feel so validated right now.

His wings flare and I think we're about to fly, but instead, he starts to fucking *glow*. He's radiating energy and it's *saturating* me. It travels in waves, out across the city and beyond, leaving in its wake a kaleidoscope of glorious colours—deep amber, rose, orange, peach and pink—they cape the city and reflect off the glassy ocean.

God-fucking damnit … and now I'm crying. I swipe at my tears and shake my head as Aero's glow subsides, though the dawn continues to bloom.

He leaves me sitting on the edge of the balcony having my tearful moment, and goes inside. Great, because I need the space. It's been a heavy turn of events.

My heart hurts.

As the dawn fades, Aero and Day come out to the balcony together, looking much less likely to throttle each other now.

"I was giving her a bath for a reason, Aero. She heals quicker than most mortals and her wounds are still filthy. I know it's hard to concentrate when the dark side takes over, something you're not used to dealing with, but if those wounds aren't cleaned, she'll end up with an infection." Day sounds, and looks, agitated. "And our mortal pet power boost will die."

Woah, zero to one fucking hundred. He could've said that to Aero inside! Arsehole. That's all I am to him, a power boost? Every time I build a little hope in Day he tears it right back down again.

"Don't you think I know that?" Aero snaps.

"Then do something about it, now, before I take her to *my* kingdom."

"Ahh no thank you. Certainly not after that stunt you just pulled on me in the bathing chamber." Fuckers got some gal.

Day's cool gaze scans over me and eventually meets my own. "Part of you enjoyed it. I know you like the way I control your body, Dell."

"What the hell makes you think that?" I snap. Presumptuous arse …

His gaze narrows. "Because, your cunt got slick when I grabbed your shoulders. I could smell it."

Ahhh … I'm speechless. And breathless. And a little wet.

A grumbling sound comes from deep within Aero's chest as Day's nostrils flare. I blush, because I know *exactly* what he's scenting … "That's it, little mortal. I intend to make her weep so much that she won't be able to see through the haze; once you stop ignoring your base urges."

Wow. Block your ears, vagina.

"You think you know me? You have no goddamn idea what's going through my mind."

He walks to the edge of the balcony and spreads his wings wide, basking in the morning glow. But the dawn doesn't suit him, not in the way *day* does. Because the dawn was made from Aero who looks fucking glorious right now.

Aero gives me a lazy smile that would shatter my heart if I had one.

Sol shrugs. "I'm sure Aero will give me an update once your mind catches up with your body. After all, Aero and I share a similar passion for pleasurable pain, and High Fae don't mind sharing … most of the time." He throws himself off the edge of the balcony and takes flight into the rising dawn, disappearing with a bright flash.

Well, fuck me.

Aero raises an eyebrow.

I roll my eyes.

I'm fucked.

Literally.

CHAPTER TEN

*Y*eah, so, Aero ends up cleaning my wounds. And now I'm fucking scared of him anew, because this is like pulling teeth. No … it's worse. Granted, we've only done one knee, we haven't even *started* on the other, or my shins, or my goddamn elbows. But hell, I think I'm done.

"For the love of dawn, Dell, sit still!"

I continue to squirm and coil like a worm stabbed with a spade, somehow managing to shift the heavy god who's half sitting on me.

Earlier, when he finally got me into the bath and examined my wounds, he realised I'd healed over too much and they needed to be re-opened and scraped clean of the filth from the dungeon floor. Not sanitary down there apparently, go figure. So now I'm tied to the motherfucking bedpost because I kept trying to gouge out Aero's eyes while he was scraping out my wounds.

Fuck you, accelerated healing. You bitch.

He brings the blade down again, this time aiming for the

scab on my shin. He's numbed the area almost to the point of entirety but it's not the pain that's affecting me, it's the fucking knife. Seeing that blade carve through my flesh … the thought of it slicing into wounds long since healed. At least visually, anyway.

I aim my knee as I coil to buck, and land it straight in Aero's groin.

Bingo, bitch.

He bellows then hisses sharply, clenching his eyes closed as he cradles his ball sack, taking deep, controlled breaths like he's in fucking labour. "I swear to God, *dear*, you're going to be the death of me." He opens his eyes and the remnants of his feral dark side seeps from the whites.

I quiver a little. Though … perhaps he could channel that energy elsewhere?

"Dell …" he warns, glowering, that marvellous body unfurling to hover over me.

My wrists are bound above my head, my only attire a light shift, something to give Aero access to the areas that needed tending.

My lips quirk up at the sides, because what I have in mind, I'm good at, whether I want to be or not. But right now, I deem it the lesser of the two evils, the worse— watching Aero carve my scabs off and scrape the imbedded filth from my flesh with a blade. No thank you.

I twist my hips, urging the shift up towards my waist and exposing the high waisted lace panties I conveniently found in one of my drawers. If Aero didn't want to see them, he wouldn't have put them in there. He only has himself to blame here.

I stretch my body out, preening like a cat and arching myself tantalisingly off the bed. Yeah, I even moan a little for impact, closing my eyes and sucking my bottom lip between my teeth like I'm caught in the throes of pleasure. I open one eye to see him watching me with a predatory, curious gaze, though his eyes are still normal. Hmm.

"Stop it. Now."

I smile. "Stop what, big boy?"

He moves forward and his eyes finally start to ink over.

Yeah, here we go …

But he stops, so close to me I can see the curl of his eyelashes. Harder to miss is the growing bulge in his tight leather pants.

Holy fuck.

Yeah, no. Fuck no.

I might've gotten a bit more than I bargained for here because I think that thing would actually rip me in half.

"It would hurt, I'm not saying it wouldn't. But you'd enjoy the pain." Aero drops the blade to the nightstand then shifts himself so he's perched, watching my body, now slack and a little frightened. Of his massive penis.

At the same time, I can feel my nether region practically drooling. Fuck you, vagina. You don't know what's good for you. But hey, I give her points for courage, though it's leading her down a direct path to an early vagina grave.

Perhaps I'll speak of her courage at her funeral. I'll be like, 'She was a brave vagina …'

Wow, I'm rambling.

Aero drops in low, bringing his mouth tantalisingly close to my ear. Or not, because I'm so scared of his penis and regretting my life decisions that now my entire body's on high alert.

"Just remember Dell," he whispers. "When your body's writhing from the inside out and you feel like you have no control, this … this was your own fault."

I gulp. Audibly. And pray to the Vagina Gods for her safe return. But then he disappears. Like … gone.

And here I am, tied to a bed made from motherfucking rose rock. I give my hands a tug, then frown.

Yeah, I might be here a while.

CHAPTER ELEVEN

"Well, well ... what do we have here?" Drake saunters in out of thin fucking air, looking all golden and dusk like.

Fuck. Fuckity fuck fuck.

I tug at my restraints, which, goddammit, are still holding fast. Screw you, Aero, and your tight sailors' knots.

Aero appears beside me. "Only if you ask nicely." He tests my restraints. "But we'll have to be quick about it, before everyone else gets here."

I almost choke. "Excuse me?"

Kal and Day turn up, looking pissed off.

"Too late," Aero drawls.

"This really is not my day," I mutter, eyeing the Sun God congregation by my bed.

"Well, not yet anyway," snaps Day, sounding a wee bit too feral for my liking.

Someone's in a bad mood. Aero probably caught him balls deep in a sea of women. I'd be pissed too if I had blue balls.

Aero suppresses a smile. Unsuccessfully.

"What are you smiling at, Dawn?" Kal asks. "Because from

where I'm standing, shit's gone really fucking downhill since you took charge."

Kal's attention is on me, scanning every inch of my body. My shift is still up around my waist because, once I got the fucker up there, I couldn't get it back down with no hands.

His brow's creased, and he's not looking at me in the way I'd expect him to be looking at me when tied to the fucking bedpost with my gear all out on display.

I clear my throat, then ask, "To what do I owe the honour?" in the most dignified voice I can muster.

"I think you know why we're here. How about you make this easy on all of us," Dusk rumbles as he steps closer to me. Actually ... as they all do.

Shit.

If Aero's penis is anything to go by, I'm either about to be torn apart four different ways, or worse, they're about to exercise their rights to clean my wounds. By force.

"Just so you all know," I state, swallowing the lump in my throat, "I kicked Aero in the balls earlier and I'm pretty sure he's infertile now. Just saying."

"It takes more than that to tamper these bad boys." Aero throws me a wink, causing the others to eye roll. Well, Drake and Kal. Day just frowns.

Right. Of course. Aero probably has a million children with his million different girlfriends, who all must have immortal vaginas that just magically pop back into place after the assault of his gigantic penis. Makes sense. Why does that thought sting? Probably because I'm barren as fuck. Yeah, that'll be why.

Aero growls under his breath, his eyes beginning to ink over as he grabs at one of my legs, copping a foot to the jaw by the one that's still free. Bullseye.

Drake stifles a laugh. Soul sister. But then he catches me watching him and frowns. Still fucked off with me, it seems.

Aero ties that foot in place to an adjacent bed pole. Day smirks and I suddenly can't move my other leg. Figures he would let Aero get kicked in the face when he could've just compelled me to lay still from the start. Arsehole. Now I can't move at all though.

"What the fuck? Why tie me if you're just going to compel me to be still anyway?" I scream, because I'm beginning to panic now.

"Precautions. Plus, I like seeing you tied to the bed," Day states with a hard gleam in his eye. Bastard.

Kal sets out equipment on a tray atop the bedside table. He takes a small bottle and tips some of the fragrant fluid onto a cloth, which he rubs all over my angry looking scabs, effectively numbing them. Aero sterilises four small blades in the fire.

Fuck.

There's sweat breaking out all over my body.

They each snatch up a blade.

Double fuck.

This is worse than getting gang banged by four feral cocksuckers with pronged schlongs.

No, wait ... that was bad.

But this situation is triggering all sorts of visuals inside my head. I'm pretty sure I'm hyperventilating ... I can't get enough air into my lungs ...

"Kal, you need to do something. Now. You should've done it as soon as you got here like we agreed," Aero snaps, as they converge, blades poised.

My eyes are darting around, moving as swiftly as my mind.

Kal bares his canines at Aero. "If you had done your job properly, we wouldn't be in this situation and I wouldn't have to be using my magic on her again. Now I'm going to be on her shit list forever. So, *fuck you.*"

Day lets out a savage growl. "Just fucking do it!"

Kal throws something heavy across the room. I don't see what, but it shatters loudly.

I seem to be causing all sorts of dramas …

Darkness.

CHAPTER TWELVE

I wake in an unfamiliar bed, bandaged.

The headboard gleams like sparkly glass. I reach back and tap it with a nail.

Ting!

Ok, not glass but something similar. Something expensive looking.

The whole room is made of the same stuff, even the floors and roof, all gleaming like the star filled night born in the day. It's stunning. Surely even a small section of that wall would be enough to fund my little life in the East ... just saying.

I tap my bandages and feel no pain. Either I've been asleep long enough for them to have healed, in which case I'm going to castrate Kal then feed his testicles to a pig, or else I'm smothered in enough of that fluid to numb the pain entirely.

Groaning, I sit up. Shit, I'm hungry. Starving in fact. I unwrap one of my arm bandages and breathe a sigh of relief. I wasn't really looking forward to castrating Kal. The wounds are clean and have healed quite a bit. Knowing my accelerated healing pace, I've probably been out for only a couple of days.

I wrap the bandage around my arm again then push the covers back, noting the white gauzy dress I'm wearing. Pretty. Whoever dressed me gets a gold star for effort. But also loses that star for seeing me naked while I was sleeping. Fucker.

I find a toilet chamber and relieve myself, then check the mirror as I'm washing my hands. What the fuck?

My cheekbones are flushed, my ivory skin gleaming in the light, and my lips appear fuller than usual; deep red and healthy looking. But most alarmingly, my wayward curls have been brushed out then placed in an elegant updo. Someone's taken more care with their unruliness than I've ever bothered to in the past.

I turn to examine the low cut of my dress, which exposes my scar ridden back in full. Well, I'm screwed if I'm going to walk around a place I know nothing about, though suspect it's the Day kingdom because it's bright as fuck, looking for food with all *that* on display. I might as well paint a giant 'R' for rebel across my motherfucking forehead. Not a good idea when the High Fae are the ones who uphold a law which suppresses women, especially Lesser Fae women, and empowers all men.

I take the shell shaped pin out of my hair and let my curls tumble down my back, covering my scars and floating down to my bum. Now, food.

After navigating a labyrinth of sparkly hallways and passing absolutely nobody, I finally stumble across the scent of food. Like a rogue hound, I follow my nose down a few flights of stairs, noting the shift of building material to stone on the third flight, just before I step into a large kitchen.

My jaw drops.

What the fuck is going on here?

The cooks are mainly men, up to their elbows in bread dough and flour or scrubbing dishes with tea towels thrown over their shoulders.

Men don't do this work, not in the Lesser Territory I come from, and as far as I was aware, not in the High Kingdoms, either. But here, females and males are working side by side, and they seem *happy* about it …

I massage my temples. Ok, so either I've lost my banana *entirely,* and this is all some complex fragment of my imagination … or I'm missing something important here. I'm thinking it's probably the latter … Sol has some explaining to do.

A smiling male with thick arms and orange stubble shadowing his jawline walks over to me, a tea towel in one hand and the plate he's drying in the other. "Need anything, luv?"

Luv? Not whore, cunt, or cum dumpster?

I stutter out something unintelligible. They probably don't recognise me as Lesser Fae, not dressed like this anyway. Granted, nobody in this kitchen has their wings out. I guess they'd get in the way, be a bit of a fire hazard and all that.

The man looks confused. "What was that, dear? Didn' quite catch it." He has an accent which accentuates his A's delightfully, his voice a roguish purr.

"Ahh, do you have anything spare to eat?" I sputter.

"Of course, luv! Why didn't ye' just say! Nex!" he bellows, and a boy with jet black hair stumbles through a door wearing an apron covered in food splatters.

"Yes, sir?" His adolescent face, rife with hormonal spots, flushes.

"The girl's starving. Get 'er a feast sorted in the dining hall. Make it quick before she eats 'er own fist."

I blush and drop my hand, nails chewed to the stubs.

Five minutes later I'm in an excessively large and very

sparkly room, one wall entirely open to the cyan ocean beyond. I'm sitting at a long table laden with lobster, steamed salmon, a bowl of root vegetables and a massive slice of cake oozing a thick, dark drizzle.

I toss pine nuts from a small bowl over the vegetables and proceed to tuck in, gorging myself like a boss for a good half hour. I finish with the cake, though by the time I'm licking the plate clean I'm so full I can hardly move, that brown sweet stuff smeared all over my face and hands. Damn, that was good. I'll probably masturbate to it later.

"I'm surprised such a small thing can eat so much food."

I sit up, on alert, gaze skimming around the room and coming to rest on Day. "How long have you been standing there?" I feel my cheeks heat. Not gonna lie, I ate that meal like an animal. I glance down at myself. Phew … no splotches on the dress. My bandages, however … aaargh.

He shrugs and pushes off from the wall, sauntering towards me with an air of bravado. This kingdom suites him, I can tell that already. "I snuck in part way through the first serving, so I got to experience the kaleidoscope of sounds you made throughout all eight servings after that. I must say, I'll dream about those sounds tonight when I'm alone in my bed."

I roll my eyes. Cock in hand; he doesn't need to say it. I was moaning like a bitch in heat throughout most of my meal. I know what that sound does to a man's, well, manhood. Hey there, soldier.

I lick the last of the drizzle from my fingers, wash it down with a chug of water then clank the glass back on the table with gusto, feeling like I could sleep for another few days now. Though, I'll probably need someone to roll me back to bed first. I yawn, almost cracking my jaw in the process, but two strong hands land on my shoulders.

"Out of the question, you've been asleep in my palace for

two days. You need sunshine. Flowers don't bloom in the dark, Dell."

I turn my head to scowl at Day over my shoulder. "What are you talking about? I saw myself in the mirror earlier and I look like a blushing goddamn bride."

His grip tightens as he leans in close. "That's because I fed you daylight, little mortal. You were starved of food, sunshine, and many other things, but I cannot replace the real thing." He gestures towards the nine empty plates before me, that were all heaped with food before I attacked them so voraciously. "Obviously. So, whether you agree to this or not, is irrelevant. I can always take you out to play by force." He pulls away, releasing my shoulders and tugging my chair back with a loud grind.

I turn on the spot. "Don't fucking damage the floor! I was eyeing that bit for my Eastern Territory fund!" That was a real pretty piece, now it's all scuffed up and will probably take a year to fucking polish.

He cocks a brow. "You were going to steal a piece of my floor?"

Oops. I slowly stand. "No … of course not."

He shakes his head, a small smile wrestling its way onto his perfect fucking lips.

"Why am I here? Did you snatch me from Aero?"

Day's eyes glint, the powder blue stark in the light. "No, he had some urgent business to attend so he couldn't babysit you, which he would if you were at his palace because he's becoming dangerously attached to our pet mortal, if missing his dawn call is anything to go by."

Wanker. I'm not a pet, least of all theirs.

He takes my wrist and tugs me towards the open wall. The sparkling metropolis lies sprawled below, a conglomeration of glittering buildings, all different heights and widths, much like a collection of shiny, pointy schlongs.

Better not say that out loud.

The cyan shoreline laps at white sandy beaches stretching as far as I can see in both directions.

I lean out, trying to see how tall the palace is. I have a sneaky suspicion Sol is trying to advertise the size of his cock with the height of his palace schlong spires. His grip on me tightens and he tugs me in.

I throw him a venomous leer. "Why are you holding me so tightly?" It's starting to fucking hurt. "Ouch!"

"Can you think of no reason?" He asks in a cutting tone that probably sends most women to their knees with his cock in their mouths.

Of course, he watched me jump off a goddam cliff. That stupid little stunt's going to follow me around for the rest of my life.

"Except for the promise of a magic boost, you don't seem like the type to care." I narrow my gaze on him. "Wait, is that why you brought me here? Because you don't give a fuck and won't go all crazy Fae on me and shirk your responsibilities?"

He tugs me a little closer and I suck in a breath, because now we're *very* close, and I'm not sure how I feel about it.

"I brought you here because of all the Sun Gods, I have the most control over my body and my mind. And … others." He looks me up and down.

My breath thickens, which I try to hide, and likely fail.

"And because I prefer not to lose track of my possessions."

I jerk my arm, but his hold is firm. Bastard. I'm nobody's bitch. Well, anymore. Unless they drop me back on Kroe's doorstep.

A mischievous glint appears in his eyes and he spreads his glorious silver wings, tugs me tightly into his chest and throws us off the balcony.

I scream then laugh as the wind whips at my face, my body tucked in against Day's muscular form. His hold on me tightens as we bank sharply, dodging our way through the cluster of pointy, sparkly, schlong towers.

They become gradually less coagulated, before we fly over the band of bleached sand, skim across the crests of the tumbling waves then drop to the water's surface, levelling out to meet with a pod of dolphins cavorting through the crystal-clear water, so close the spray from their play dances across my skin. We race ahead of the dolphins, flying so fast now the wind catches my laughter and whips it away before it leaves my lips.

But those *wings*. My vagina wants to rub herself all over them, though I'm trying my hardest to block her running commentary on how big and shiny they are. She's weeping with delight that she's getting to see them up close and personal again, and it's really distracting. I wish she'd keep her happy vagina tears to herself.

I'm starting to think the Sun Gods are enjoying parading their massive godly wings around for me, flashing them about and pumping at the air. If I see another pair of Sun God wings in the not too distant future, I might just have a coronary. My vagina's eager to rise to the occasion, but personally, I could barely handle *one* High Fae, let alone four High Fae fucking *Sun Gods.* It might actually kill me. Immortals have too much stamina for my little mortal vagina, even if she does consider herself a thoroughbred.

I glance back at the city, which backs onto an impressive mountain range that's all lush and fertile beneath the bright rays of the midday sun. And I confirm, Sol's palace spires are fucking *huge.* My vagina just fainted, but Sol's grip tightens and she rouses immediately from her dramatic, temporary exit. I wiggle a little so he loosens his hold, not so much that he'll drop me, that wouldn't be fun, but enough so my vagina can recover and regain her limited mental capacity.

I breathe in a large dose of sea air. Yeah, I must admit, the sunshine on my face feels damn glorious.

"You're relaxing," Day states.

I twist my head around to look at him. "Am I not meant to be? I thought that's what you wanted?" High maintenance Fae God.

He smiles. "It is what I want, I'm just not used to your scent smelling as such. It's nice."

Nice? Well, fuck me. I never thought I'd hear *that* word come out of his controlling, sadistic mouth. I shift my gaze back to the ocean. "I made it down to the kitchen earlier, —"

"I noticed."

"*And,*" I continue, glaring at him. I should probably die for that, but he only arches a brow, and I carry on, like a boss. "I noticed both men *and* women working the kitchen. Why?"

A beat passes, then another, before Day spins me around so I'm now facing him. His expression is hard, his eyes a little inked, but they quickly return to normal. He searches my face, finally shaking his head. "I shouldn't be able to tell you this. It doesn't make any fucking sense."

"Tell me what?"

"I don't abide by the King's rules where I can avoid it—nor does my Kingdom. Same goes for Dawn, Dusk and Night. I don't give a fuck that the world gave birth to him and his pure white fucking wings. That dove-man is a psychopath and one day, I will kill him."

Well, fuck, that was a slap to the labia.

"*Kill him?* Isn't he integral for the world to … to … I don't know, stay *round* or some shit?"

"All he's doing is poisoning the world that gave him life. Can't you tell it's rotting? It's people along with it? I know you haven't seen much beyond that shit smeared city, but the land is withering, just like his ancient, ungodly mind."

Fuck. I feel the blood draining from my face, my vagina

ducking under the covers as my heart begins to gallop in my chest. This is ... a lot.

I shake my head. It doesn't make sense ...

"Why haven't any of us on the mortal lands heard of this?" My voice is hoarse, because if it's true, this is ground-breaking. For many.

For me.

He frowns. "Why would he tell anyone on the mortal lands? All that would do is plant a seed of doubt in everyone's mind. Spark rebellions. Not that much could be achieved from the slums the mortal lands have become, but still ... he may be a psycho, but he's no idiot."

"I didn't mean him, Sol! Four gods against one? I know the King's powerful, but from what I've seen, so are you four! Why the fuck don't you tell anyone?" I'm yelling now, because the beast inside me is well and truly perched and ready to pounce. Her target—the God of fucking Day.

His gaze narrows, nostrils flaring as his chest tightens against my body. "Don't you think we would if we could? Don't you think we've *tried*? We're powerless! We're *nothing* compared to what we used to be, Dell; practically fucking shadows of ourselves. You have *no* idea what we've lost! What we continue to lose every fucking day because of that immortal bastard who doesn't deserve the title of God!"

He's yelling. Guess it's contagious. Fury's rolling off him in waves, causing my vagina to shrivel up, even from her little spot beneath the covers. Fucking pussy. I harden my features to make up for her incompetence.

"He's cast a ward, causing everyone to forget the binding phrase; the words you used to summon us the day you threw yourself off the cliff." The bastard's having a jab.

"You want to go there again, Sol?"

He hisses at me. Savage.

"We are fucking there! You shouldn't have been able to

use them! You shouldn't have gotten that fucking wish in the first place!"

Yikes. Feral, growly Sol is in full swing.

"Those words are special, Dell. They are the key to the give and take of power between the beings born of this world, and the sun. Or *us* as it's representatives. Without them, we haven't been able to restore our energy, our *anchor* which holds us here. Not only that, we've been forced to control the sun with our stores, which are running dangerously low."

Yeah, wow ... okay.

This is too much to take in. I'm feeling a little nauseous. Actually ... a *lot* nauseous.

"He's warded us against speaking of, or even *representing* such things outside our kingdoms. In our weakened states, going against those wards would actually *kill* us. *That's* why everyone thinks we're on his fucking side, mortal."

Kill them? Fucking hell—this is too much. I don't want to hear more, but I can't bring myself to stop him either ...

He shakes his head, then arches his neck left and right, as if he's working to expel some of the tension coiling his muscles. "Our territories used to be split four ways, evenly across the globe. There are *physical* markers that represent the old boundaries. Though he's incredibly powerful, we resided in harmony for thousands of years *with* King Sterling, caring for our people, and our world, *together*. But something changed and he got sick of sharing. Now our people, who don't have access to the Bright like us Gods do, are literally walled off in our kingdoms." He tugs me closer to his body, crushing me against him, fuelling my concern that I'm about to vomit all over the man. "If King Sterling knew we were dragging a mortal through the Bright to get her around, we would get spit roasted."

A Sun God spit roast sounds fucking delectable, but you didn't hear it from me.

His gaze shifts from my face, to the horizon. "He's stronger than ever, so are his wards. We still hold power over and around our kingdoms, but even that diminishes daily, the wards tugging closer every fucking hour as we slowly lose the ability to fight them."

No wonder they're so desperate for a power surge. No wonder they're so desperate to keep me safe.

"What ... what happens when your power runs out entirely?"

The muscles in his jaw tense and he stares ahead, not meeting my gaze. "He'll take our wings, and we'll fall."

Motherfucker.

"And the sun cycle?" I choke out the words, afraid of the answer, but needing to know.

There's a pause and our gazes lock, his wings beating in rhythm to my pounding heart.

"He thinks the world can survive without it, without us. My guess is Kal, Drake, Aero and I will be absorbed by the sun again, and the world will perish, along with every mortal *and* immortal living here." He shrugs. "Like I said, a flower doesn't bloom in the dark, Dell."

I'm going to vomit. My mouth starts filling with saliva. Yeah, definitely going to vomit.

"Mortal?"

I shake my head, covering my mouth with my hand, because the last thing I want to do is projectile vomit all over those beautiful fucking wings. We're suddenly whisked into the Bright so quickly that the nausea strengthens twice fold, but then I'm landing on sand, before a bush. I part the branches and proceed to empty my guts. Repeatedly.

Why did I eat so much? That cake with the gooey drizzle does *not* taste good coming up the other way. It's not until I think I've finished that I notice the hands holding my hair at the nape of my neck. Nice. Brownie points for Sol. "Thanks," I croak, pushing the bush back into position and wiping my mouth.

I'm about to try and stand when I'm suddenly swept up against Sol's chest and carried towards the sound of lapping waves. I look around and see that we're on an island, one so small I could walk thirty paces from one shore to the other in either direction. There's a rustic little hut in the centre of the island, white curtains billowing softly in the wind. The building's fringed with palm trees heavy with coconuts, and a few bushes—one of which has a pool of vomit beneath it, but we'll ignore that minor detail.

Sol places me feet first into the crystal-clear water. It's tepid, I want to get in. No ... I *need* to get in. I take a shaky step forward, but Sol's holding my arms.

"I want to swim." I glance back at him. "Please don't stop me."

He's frowning. "You're fully dressed and in a weakened state—it'll be dangerous. You either take the dress off or you don't go in at all."

I know he's right, but it doesn't stop me from rolling my eyes. Is it possible he's concerned for my actual life rather than just his power boost? "Fine then. Turn around." To my surprise, he does.

With the dress gone, I'm left wearing only bandages and my high waisted underwear, but at least my scar's covered.

I dive in, relishing the sensation of the water dancing along my skin as I make my way into the depths, my body skimming through the water, unperturbed by the small waves. I surface, lick my lips, savouring the salty tang, the taste of freedom.

I need to be under again. I need to be deep. I need to

drown everything that's playing out in my head. Closing my eyes, I dive.

Visuals, too many visuals. Too many thoughts I'm trying to suppress. It's like tearing open an old wound, and it hurts like hell.

Suppress. Suppress.

Because Aero can hear my fucking thoughts. Because I can't escape even though I tried. Even though I know I'll never be good enough.

Opening my eyes, I push myself deeper. The light fades as I descend and the temperature cools. It's a small release, a place for me to scream, and I do. Bubbles cascade about my face and make a mad dash for the surface, searching for their own freedom.

I hover, lungs exasperated, controlling them. Don't panic. Control. Control.

I ignore the shadow circling above. I know it's not a shark. It's Sol; a predator of another kind. But not the sexual predator I initially thought him to be. He doesn't realise it yet, but he's hunting me. Just not in the way you might expect.

How the fuck have I ended up here? I push myself to the surface, take deep, gasping breaths, then descend again. And scream into the ocean. Again and again I dive and scream. The water does not judge, she probably doesn't even hear me. I'm okay with that because sometimes you just need to let it out.

My mind is heavy, but for once, my body's not. For once my body represents nothing. For once it's not barren, broken, and defiled. Until it fails me, becoming tired and weak, and I must go in.

I continue to ignore the shadow hovering as I swim to shore. When I reach the sand, arms covering my boobs, Sol lands before me, gaze wary. Perhaps he knows not to prod a dragon, because that's what I am right now, and there is one thing I need to do today.

One.

It's likely not going to go down too well, which is why I need to choose the right moment.

I pick up my dress and drag it on over my wet skin, then walk past Sol towards the shack while unravelling the sodden bandages from my arms. As I climb the creaking stairs, I run my hand along the sandy rail that's chipped and faded, the rough sawn edge scratching at the scar on my palm.

I breathe my first unrestricted breath since Sol bombed me with information, because this place reminds me of home. The home I shared with my mother. It's simple and ordinary. Aged but treasured. It's just a feeling … but I know it in my heart. This place is loved. Loved like I was. Once.

Walking through the gap where a door might have been, I take in the rustic charm of my surroundings before sitting on the edge of the large bed parked against the far wall. The linen is fresh and white, pillows plump and inviting. I put the bandages aside and grasp two handfuls of the bedding, fists clenched so tightly my hands go numb.

Finally, I let go.

Let go, Dell.

Let. Go.

I gasp out a breath I didn't realise I was holding as Sol walks inside, expression cautious, as though he's approaching a wounded animal.

Fuck, he has no idea just how wounded I am.

"Are … you ok?"

"No." Not now. Not since I was four. Perhaps not even before then, but at least the illusion was there.

After a pause he nods, placing his hands in his pockets and looking towards his feet. He draws a deep breath. "I'm not too good at the whole … emotional thing. That's why I brought you here, to my sanctuary. I'd hoped it would speak for itself …" He looks around, assessing, appearing to distract himself.

I like this place more than I feel comfortable saying right now. I like to think one day I'll be able to tell him how close it feels to my own heart. One day when I'm not so fucked up.

His gaze meets mine, and it's all hard edges again. All control. All Sol. "What do you need from me right now?"

To be left alone—forever. To lose my mind entirely. Both things I know are unobtainable. Unless I give myself a fucking lobotomy, and to be honest, I'm not even sure that's possible. I lift my chin. "I want you to take me back to Grueling. There's something there I need to retrieve."

"Out of the fucking question."

I frown. "You asked me what I need, and this is what I fucking need!" My voice has a frantic rawness to it, because I've finally voiced the fact that I've left something crucial in that place where people lose themselves in more ways than one.

He shifts so fast he's a blur—shoving me backwards onto the coverlet. His half-naked body hovers, so close I can feel his heat washing over me in waves, causing my underappreciated nipples to harden. My breathing comes deeply, my heart pounding in my ears.

"You don't get it, little mortal. Aero and I, for the most part, have a good relationship. We talk." He takes my hand in his own and flashes my scarred palm in my face. "I know what they fucking did to you there. I'll never let you go back."

He drops my hand and brings his face closer to mine, until we're mixing harsh breaths. Will to fucking will. He has no idea just how rock solid mine is though.

"Never." His teeth are bared and very fucking close to my neck.

A TOKEN'S WORTH

I was hoping this would go down a little more smoothly. Damnit. I lift my chin and steady my breathing. "I wish for you to take me back to Grueling for an hour."

He can't come with me, can't be seen to be helping a mortal female without the implications of the King's wards. Which is good, because this is something I must do on my own.

Sol growls, eyes widening, shoulder muscles coiling. A wave of magic washes over my skin as he studies me, canines extended, his body trembling. "Do you have a death wish, girl?"

I keep my gaze trained on the man I thought I could read, the man I know know has many more layers than I initially suspected.

Like me, I guess.

I hope like hell those layers won't come back to haunt me … especially as I go back to the doors of death to retrieve the relics of my past.

"Not a death wish. I'm just taking charge of my life."

Because I may not have the capabilities to save the world, but I'm done being someone else's bitch.

CHAPTER THIRTEEN

"You have one fucking hour," Sol snaps, frowning at my disguise—a red cape with a pillow stuffed down my front. Nothing to see here, folks.

"Don't forget, I'm fucking warded here. I can't even *attempt* to save your arse if there are other eyes around, unless I want to die, which I don't. Nor do I want my brothers to die. So you better make sure you're by yourself when the hour's up so I can get you the fuck out of this shit smeared city. Do you understand, Dell?"

Wow. Serious tone.

"I understand. I understood the first seven times you told me, too. I can handle myself, alright?"

He rolls his fucking eyes at me before flying away through the dull morning light, leaving me alone in Hind Meadow on the outskirts of Grueling.

"Moody Fae God." I start walking towards the smell of dirty street water and rotting fish, pushing up the hood of my cloak to cover my hair and most of my face. Reaching the city, I pass painted ladies—wearing corsets pushing their breasts up to their chins and hailing the few men who meander along the muddy footpaths.

I look down at my disguise and smile. Sol thought it was a terrible idea, I did it anyway.

The men wear fancy silk blouses and breeches pulled so high up their arses I'm surprised they can walk. Red sashes are bound tightly around their waists, red to show their loyalty to King Sterling. *His* colour, even though his own wings are fucking white.

I shuffle past unnoticed because I'm disguised as a pregnant breeder. Fucking genius, I know. I could be carrying a blessed boy! Nobody's going to touch me with a ten-foot penis in this red cape.

Women all wear red; the breeders—capes, the whores—skirts, the same as the help because really, what's the difference? We all get preyed on, except the breeders; Fae who possess the right characteristics, looks or heritage to play the part.

The breeders get treated a lot better most of the time, except that the newborns are taken away as soon as they can survive off the tit—to be brought up by the sperm donor that spawned the Faeling if it's a boy. If it's a girl, they're marked for future potential breeders or sold to the highest bidder at the weekly market place.

My destiny was determined when Kroe found me that day, four years old, walking the streets covered from head to toe in my mother's blood. He hid me for years in the basement, in the dark, waiting for me to develop breasts and womanly curves ripe for fucking, hiding his pretty little 'Cupcake' so I didn't get noticed … snatched up as a potential breeder.

I started to bleed when I was nine, managed to hide it for three years with the help of an older woman who was kind to me. Marion knew which herbs to give me to cease the monthly bleeding, and she taught me how to tend my own wounds after the regular beatings to 'tame my feral soul.'

Then she stopped coming, replaced by a deaf woman who had no tongue.

Locked in the dark with my chamber pot and small collection of relics to keep me company, I had no access to herbs to continue the treatment. It didn't take long for Kroe to catch on, to see the blood on my sheets and to haul me to the fucking surgeon.

I've been highly sought after over the years, having the supposed beauty of a breeder and the barren body of someone you can shag to your heart's content with no risk of breeding implications. Someone to work out your wildest fantasies on, who'll look good while you're maiming her. Just don't fuck up her face, then you'll pay a handsome fee.

I'm receiving the odd curious look, so I tug my hood tighter around my face—not far to go now.

The box I'm looking for is hidden beneath a rock in the dungeon that was my home for seven years. The place where darkness was my only companion, apart from my master who fucked me and the woman who healed me.

Somehow, I need to get in there.

By the grace of fuck knows, I make it to the long alleyway next to Kroe's castle-like establishment, the largest and most lavish building in Grueling, three storeys tall and made entirely of stone.

I reach the low-lying window that's at knee level, but has a dirty great big puddle on the ground right beside it. Of course. The window's barred but one of them is loose, it can be pulled away and replaced at will. It took me four years to saw through that fucker with a contraband butter knife when I was supposed to be sleeping. Back then when I had hope.

I'd heard from one brazen woman that a few had escaped and travelled East, where they were living happily, making homes in the trunks of the ancient trees. Problem is the East is across a goddamn desert that's a two-week camel ride if you can afford it. Even if you have the money, no man would sell a whore a fucking camel. How do I know this? I tried. And failed. And got severely fucking beaten for my efforts, time and again.

I finally gave up and muted my soul.

I stuff the pillow and robe in a crate on the opposite side of the alley. Hopefully I'll need them on my way out again. I hike up my skirt, tiptoe around the puddle of piss and grip at the loose bar, wriggling it to displace it. It falls into my hand with the harsh scrape of metal on metal. I wince. It's around six in the morning and winter in this part of the world, so it's still quiet. Kroe's girls don't usually do overnight shifts, because he works us so hard during the day since his is the number one place to get laid. Everyone *should* be still sleeping. I'd like it to stay that way.

I slip into the small space, contorting my limbs to fit between the bars. It's not that difficult because I'm flexible as fuck, if I do say so myself.

Once inside the room I realise I dropped the hem of my skirt in the puddle and I now smell like a toilet that hasn't been flushed for weeks. Repressing the urge to gag, I wring it out and end up with hands smelling the same. Fucking lovely.

This room's used for storage, and it's dark enough to make things difficult, if I didn't know my way around. I shuffle a few feet to the right, past the piano, avoiding the tall lampshade that jingles. A small step to the left, turn my body to the right and ease past the two bookcases wedged closely together. I climb over the large blanket box, trying not to touch the two chairs that are upside down on top of it, then pause because there are fucking footsteps in the hall outside the room...

Not ideal. Not fucking ideal.

Perhaps they heard me prying the bar from the window? Shit. Getting caught is certainly not on the top of my priority list. For one, Sol would probably revel in the glory of being right about this whole scenario, and I'd never live it down. Not to mention I'd be dragged back into the throngs of eternal fuckery.

With the stealth of a cockroach, I climb backwards over the blanket box, shuffle between the two bookcases and nestle myself beneath a small coffee table that's covered in about an inch of dust. My nose instantly starts to itch. Yeah, not the best time to have a fucking dust allergy.

The door to the storage basement swings open and the familiar scent of cigars and brandy infuses my senses.

Fuck. Fucking fuckity fuck.

Kroe whistles a familiar tune, the same one I've heard him hum many times before—mainly post fuck while he wiped the cum from my leg and backside, and the underside of his limp cock.

The room brightens and I realise he's carrying a lantern, illuminating his way through the junk. He shuffles a few pieces around as though he's looking for something, then it goes quiet, as if he's standing still... listening.

My nose itch peaks like a brewing orgasm, my eyes watering as I suppress the sneeze that's desperate to shoot its load all over my motherfucking hand.

He takes a step in my direction, then another. He's so close I can hear him breathing, drawing a deep lungful of air.

I hold my breath.

The bastard's probably scenting me. The same way I just scented him.

I squeeze my eyes shut. I'm fucked. And then I'll be fucked. And then I'll probably fucking die.

He draws down another whiff of the room. "Smells like piss in here," he states, then continues with his rummaging.

And even though my foul odour just saved me from falling back into a life of fuckery, my face heats, because he's right ... I do smell like a fucking toilet.

I take a small, shaky breath because I just dodged the whipping post—something I'm historically not very good at. But the battle isn't won yet, because all that blood rushing to my face is bringing forth another mind-blowing, orgasmic sneeze. And I want it. I want it bad. I want it so bad that I'm considering just letting the fucker fly.

I wonder if I could make it out through my little escape gap before he would reach me? Doubtful. He'd probably catch me by the ankles and I'd fall vagina first back into this hole of a life.

Shit.

Tears are streaming down my face from the effort of keeping the fucker reined in. I'm not crying, my body's just seeping juices unceremoniously.

"There you are," Kroe mumbles, before dragging something along the ground. He blows a breath over whatever the hell it is, sending plumes of dust billowing into the air.

Fuck.

I'm holding my breath, fingers clamping my nose with my eyes screwed shut, because that's all I can do to avoid this undoubtedly mind-blowing sneeze.

He opens the door and drags what sounds like a dead fucking body through it, before allowing the door to thump shut behind him.

I don't dare let out my breath. Not yet. Not until I hear him pass through the door at the top of the stairway. By the time he drags whatever the hell he came down here for up to the top of those stairs I'm damn near close to passing out.

Finally I breathe, and the sneeze comes out the second I open my mouth, which feels fucking amazing, because it's not one sneeze, it's two, right the fuck on top of each other. I bury my head in my skirt that smells like a toilet to tamper the sound, then gag, instantly regretting it. This is not my day.

I shuffle out from under the table, edge myself back between the bookcases and clamber over the top of the blanket box, before tiptoeing across the room to the doorway Kroe just took. I take a moment to consider my questionable life choices before I gently pry it open, mainly concentrating on those stairs to the right, which lead to Kroe's personal quarters, and check for any sign of life.

None. Good.

There isn't much light without my usual lantern down here, which is a good thing, though the hallway looks like it belongs in a haunted house. I hope no ghosts sneak up and try to fornicate with me.

Now for the hard part—I need to quietly pry open that trap door right there, a few metres down the hallway to the left. If someone comes down those stairs, I'm fucked. If I make too much noise lifting the heavy trap door, I'm fucked. If somebody randomly decides to lock the fucking latch while I'm down there, I'm fucked.

No big deal.

I take a deep breath, then another, and go for it.

It's not until I have the fifty-kilogram door lifted half way up that I realise I may not have the strength to push the fucker back open from the inside once I'm down there. Usually I leave it open when I'm visiting. Can't fucking do *that* today.

I come down here often because I like to visit my things,

and I can disguise that by telling Kroe I want to visit my 'home'. He gets some sick sense of pleasure from it, I see it in his eyes and I'm not entirely repulsed by the thought. Probably because I'm fucked in the head too, because of the seven years I spent knowing nothing except the darkness, his penis, and the healing hands of Marion.

I'm gritting my teeth as I crawl through the gap, all the while keeping the trap door hoisted. I manoeuvre my body, dangling my feet through the hole so I can gain leverage on the ladder positioned there. I hope this isn't the moment I drop a trap door at an inconsequential time and lose a fucking finger.

And no, it isn't, because I manage to close it quietly without losing leverage or making a single noise. I'm awesome, I'll never underestimate myself again. If I wasn't me already, I'd wish I were me, because that was legendary. I fist pump the air and wave to my imaginary, cheering crowd.

Thank you. Thank you.

I get to the bottom of the ladder and start blowing kisses to them while I smile and wave, because they're cheering so fucking loudly. I love my fans.

"What the fuck is she doing?"

I freeze. Shit. That was Drake. I turn in the direction of his voice but can't see *anything*, because it's pitch black in here.

Someone sparks a lantern and Drake in all his golden glory, enhanced further by the lantern light, comes into view. He has his arms crossed over his chest, looking royally pissed.

But who the shit is holding the lantern?

I turn, and there's Kal looking sultry as fuck, even with that frown on his face and hip wide stance. His right hand is in his pocket, but I can see that it's balled into a fist. Either that or he's very glad to see me.

"Why the fuck are *you guys* here?" I hiss, because I'm pissed off. My little 'home' is just through that brass door over there, and I can't have my moment with my box if these two hulking arseholes are looming over me like persistent fucking shadows.

"Why do you think, mortal?" Drake asks.

"Fucking Aero." I moan, slapping my palm to my face. That bastard's been listening to my thoughts this entire time. I need to rein in my internal vomit.

Drake nods, his loose curls flicking before his eyes. He casually swipes them away before taking two steps towards me. "Bingo."

I hold my ground because this isn't fair. I'm so close. "Why didn't *he* come then?"

Drake frowns. "Because that fucker's lost a lot of control since you came on the scene, and we couldn't risk drawing attention to ourselves right now. So, Sol intervened."

Right.

"Meaning he compelled him to stand still like a fucking statue. Bet that's going down like a bag of shit." I don't do the family dynamics any favours.

I turn to Kal, who suits all this darkness I'd like to add, though he's still on my shit list. "So, have you guys come to take me?" My tone's flat, because I feel flat. My imaginary crowd's throwing vegetables.

Kal grinds his jaw. "No."

"Why not?" That piqued my interest, and my crowd's murmuring. There are a lot of them so it's loud as fuck. Shh guys, I need to hear.

Kal shuffles, all those hard muscles seeming to flex as if he's restraining himself. "Because we *can't*."

Ahh … "Say what now?"

"Mouth fucking closed Kal, you idiot!" Drake snaps.

But then it hits me like a penis to the rear end. "The wish.

You guys can't interfere until my hour's up either … can you?"

Kal pulls his fist from his pocket and rubs at his face, probably because he can't fucking lie to me, none of them can, something I haven't utilised enough. The movement makes him appear exhausted, and a little bit tousled, which makes me think about dancing the maypole with him. Wayward vagina.

"No," Drake snaps.

I turn my attention to him. He's all up in my personal space and needs to take a step the fuck back, because he can't do anything. Which means I'm still a free woman.

"Boom, bitches," I say, dropping an imaginary sound amplifier. My entire crowd are having simultaneous orgasms, and I applaud them for living their best lives in the light of this glorious moment.

The men hiss at me as I snatch Kal's lantern and saunter towards the brass door with as much hip sway as I can muster. But when I reach the door I peer back over my shoulder at them. "Don't come through here," I say, all humour gone from my voice. "I'm not telling, I'm asking. This is a private place. I'll only be a moment."

Not only that, even with the door closed I can scent those seven years I spent in there seeping through the grate in the door. I was hoping to avoid bringing anyone else down here … but my gods are disobedient bastards who can't take a hint.

To my surprise, they don't argue. Instead, I receive two clipped nods from two tight jawed Fae Gods who are eyeing me like I'm the candy their mummy told them they couldn't have until after dinner time. It's kind of correct, except they must work their way off my shit list before they can lick me all over. My vagina's purring at the prospect, especially because my Fae Gods are all obedient right now, but I ignore her because she's got a dirty mind and it's distracting.

I crank the handle of the door, the brass biting cold in my palm, and shove it open. It's a heavy door, with only a two-foot square grate for me to catch a peep through, though at such a young age I was too small to reach it. Once I grew tall enough, imagine my disappointment when I realised it was so fucking dark in the catchment room, I couldn't see anything anyway. Yeah, that shit will break your spirit more than most other forms of torture.

My body goes hot all over as I step into the gloom, into the lingering stench of all the fuckery this room has seen. I draw a deep breath of coppery, stagnant air to still my heart that's beating faster than a man with his cock in his hand, before I turn and push the door—not so it closes, just so I have some motherfucking privacy.

The men are shuffling around outside, but I ignore them. They can surely take care of themselves. I mean hell, the goddamn sun made them after all.

I pan my lantern and my vision around the room, past the small iron bed bolted to the ground. How the fuck didn't I catch something deadly sleeping on that half rotten mattress all those years? Actually, I guess I did ... my mind's probably more rotten than the mattress.

My artistries are carved into the walls, large and small images of my mother, dug into the stone using the edge of my metal spoon via the meagre lantern light post meal times. It was hard when she never really looked like a person, but it was her essence that I drew.

And that's it, that's all there is. Apart from my chamber pot over there. My little four by four, a place I could scream as loud as I was able, and nobody would hear me. Or perhaps they did hear me, and just never came.

I walk to the bed, ignoring the numerous blood stains

splattered across the floor. They always give me the creeps. Crouching, I push myself beneath the bed, catching an unexpected whiff of dust and sneezing so hard I'm not entirely certain my panties are still dry, knocking my chin on the stone floor in the process. "Ow!" Fucking dust. I'll smite you, little fuckers.

"Everything all right in there?" Drake asks. His voice sounds like an adolescent boy with pitch problems for some reason. Now I'm picturing him as a sexy teenager with that mass of golden curls and enough raging hormones to fuck me into a coma. Is that bad? Probably. Though I'm talking very, very late teens here. I'm no sicko. I wonder if his penis is the size of Aero's?

Wow, that was a roller coaster. Now my vaginas distracted from the task at hand and it's an effort to rein the bitch in. I haven't had any time alone with her lately, perhaps that's her problem. I make note to make a date with my wayward vagina, who's obviously crying out for attention.

"Dell?" Drake whisper-yells through the grate, and the sound jolts me out of my mind funk.

"I'm fine!" I whisper-yell back. "Overbearing Fae bastard," I mumble, noting the blood dripping from my chin. I wipe it away, frowning at the smear on the back of my hand. Another fucking scar.

I finger around the edges of the large, heavy brick, the one with bloody hearts painted on it. Why hearts, you ask? Fuck knows, I'm not sentimental like that. They were just fun to draw when I got bored one day.

Wedging it free, I lift it from the ground, difficult from such a shitty vantage point. Once it's out of the way, I reach inside the exposed cavity I dug out many years ago. I needed somewhere to hide my bits, the ones that were hidden in the pockets of my cape when Kroe found me that day. I couldn't leave them behind ... as well as everything else.

My hand clamps around my wooden box, the one Marion gave me when she snuck me some herbs to chew that were supposed to ward off the sickness of the dark. I didn't die so I guess they worked. I pull the box out and sigh with relief.

I got it. I fucking got it.

My hands itch to rifle through the contents, to see those parts of myself again.

"If you don't come out of there soon, I'm going to drag you out by your fucking ankles," Drake hisses through the grate.

I huff loudly and shuffle backwards out from under the bed, bum in the air. If they wanted to, they could come in, pull the door shut, hoist my skirt up over my hips and take me right now. Easily. In fact, they've had plenty of opportunities. The fact that they haven't taken them makes me simultaneously dubious of them and want to fuck them senseless. And that's me talking, not my vagina. I'm not sure what to think of men who don't trip into my vagina, penis first, if given the opportunity.

I clamber up, wiping at my dripping chin and ignoring the two pairs of hooded eyes watching me through the grate. Creepy. The door swings open for me and I step out, handing Kal the lantern and placing the box in my large pocket. I now have two boxes in my skirt that need tending to. I'm going to be a busy girl.

"Did you get what you came for?" Drake drawls, like I'm inconveniencing him with my presence. Fucker.

"Yes, I did. And now I'm going to find a dark little corner where I can finger my bits."

Kal quirks a brow and Drake takes a step closer. I wave the immature bastards away.

"Not my lady bits, get your minds out of the gutter."

I walk towards the ladder but a large hand wraps around

my elbow, instantly halting me. I scowl over my shoulder and follow the arm back to Drake, who smirks at me.

"Not so easy, Dell. You're staying right here until that fucking hour is up."

"Like fuck."

They growl at me, like dogs. Cute. It doesn't frighten me at all right now, because they're all bark and no potential for bite until my well-earned hour is up. And even then, they can't do anything if I'm in the presence of even one regular city folk, unless they want to die, because they're warded not to draw attention to their rebellious ways.

My terms now, fuckers. Oh, how the tables have turned.

I whip my arm from his grasp.

Drake's all about control, I think. This must be a real struggle for him, wanting to have his way but being completely powerless to stop me from walking out like a boss. Which is what I'm about to do, because I've had enough of this place. Now that I have my things, I'm done. I won't be back.

I throw Drake a wink and saunter up the ladder. I must be mad, nobody else would dare to piss off a god they're all out of wishes with. The odds are not in my favour because he still has one of his own, and I'm best to just avoid Drake's company altogether, especially since my vagina's still reeling from his *nearly* orgasmic pleasure play the other day.

Speaking of which, best not remind him of that. I probably have about seventeen or so minutes left on my current wish ticker—once that runs out, and he gets me alone, Drake will probably fuck me right up. And down. And up again. I'll probably even enjoy it because I'm a psychological mess with a wayward vagina.

A hand grasps around my ankle and I'm thrown into a sea of white, before we emerge right in another fucking piss puddle in the alleyway outside Kroe's. Kal and Drake are on either side of me, but I note they've magically avoided the golden puddle I'm currently ankle-deep in. They glance at my feet with twin smirks I want to smack off their perfect fucking faces. Arseholes.

"Why the shit did you land me in piss?"

Drake shrugs. "Someone was shifting stuff from the storage room, so it wasn't safe for you to exit through the trapdoor. Figured if we landed you in piss nobody would want to touch you even if you walk through the centre of town for the next fifteen minutes." He takes a whiff of me, scrunches his nose, then takes a step backwards. Kal does the same. "Seems it worked."

Here I was thinking I was in the company of men with thousands of years worth of accumulated immortal grace. Obviously, I was mistaken.

"I'm going back to the meadow," I state, turning to start the back way around the building so I can collect my robe and pillow. "Unless you want to draw attention to yourselves, I would stay the fuck back. Just saying." I have fourteen more minutes of supposed pregnant freedom, then the bastards will probably do everything in their power to get me away from any crowds so they can zap me out of here. I'm going to make the most of it while I can.

They follow me, upwind, probably because I smell like a dirty toilet, around to the alley on the other side of the building where I proceed to wrap my cape around my shoulders then stuff the pillow down my blouse—adjusting it so it looks believable.

"What's that?" Kal asks, a hint of amusement in his voice.

"It's a fantastic fucking disguise, that's what it is," I say with conviction, staring down my nose while primping the folds of red velvet coating my rounded belly. I glance up and catch Drake scratching at his chin with his thumb and forefinger, studying me. "What's your problem?"

He shrugs. "I'm just thinking we may need to roll you in more piss now that you have an extra layer on."

I glare at him. If he's not careful, even my vagina's going to decide his penis isn't worth the effort. I turn and walk down the alley before he thinks too hard on the piss topic, though. I wouldn't put it past them to whip down their trousers and pee all over me like dogs marking their territory.

CHAPTER FOURTEEN

Grueling's quiet at the arse crack of dawn. Most of the time. Except when there's some sort of public punishment planned, then the square teems with people, all frothing for the carnage about to unfold.

I've been the one on that dais before. The one in the middle of the square over there, about two and a half meters high and currently surrounded by people, men and women both. The dais is made of wood—unfortunate because wood absorbs blood. No matter how much that fucker gets scrubbed, the stains of the whipped and brutalised will never fully fade.

My blood's on there, from more than one occasion.

Most people with more than one strike against their name lose their head. I think my affiliation with Kroe has granted me more leeway than most. I have the scars to show for it.

It's not me up there today though. It's some fresh-faced, petite, mousey haired girl I've never seen before that's suspended between two men by her spindly arms. She's young, too young, and she looks frightened.

A TOKEN'S WORTH

Is that ...? Yes. It's Kroe's mark on her motherfucking palm, raised and angry red, as if she was branded recently. She's probably the latest recruit to fill the void left by me while I've been gorging myself on freedom, comfortable beds, and sexy High Fae Gods.

Fuck.

Internal moral dilemma right there.

She's like a poster girl for degradation, pleading straight to my vulnerable righteous side that I've spent the last number of years repressing. And it's hurting. It's hurting like a motherfucker.

Her eyes trail the man walking back and forth before her, testing the air with a fucking cat o' nine tails whip, making a loud snapping sound. I haven't had that one before, it looks like a nasty bastard.

She's whimpering, leaking fluids left, right and centre. Tears, snot, spit ... there's even something wet pooling down the front of her skirt. Poor girl, I pissed myself the first time too.

I look around for Kroe, whose nowhere to be seen. Bastard sent her to the whipping post, probably for crying during sex with a customer or some shit and doesn't even have the decency to watch. Arsehole.

I see Kal and Drake hidden in the shadows of a two-story building, away from the assaulting morning light, hooded capes pulled over their faces. Not sure where the fuck they acquired *them* from. Drake signals for me to sink into the shadows of the building I'm standing by, and I do so, only so they'll stop fucking focusing on me and give me space to think, because my head's in a jumble right now.

One of the fucktards on the dais tugs the girl's skirt off her frail body, before roughly untying her corset, exposing what little bust she has.

A thick swell of nausea rolls over me, because her panties

are drenched in blood, which is now dribbling down the front of her thighs. I think she's just had the fucking spoon treatment, and she's obviously torn her stitches from all the struggling she's been doing. They rip her underwear from her body and my suspicions are confirmed.

Fuck this.

I'm taking my cape off and removing my fake fucking pregnancy before I can take my next breath or even *consider* a game plan, because beneath the surface I'm a repressed impulsive bitch.

I move forward swiftly, landing myself amongst a small group of women, because I have a goddamn box in my skirt pocket that's weighing heavily on my conscience, and I can't take that to the fucking dais with me.

'Aero?' I think-yell.

A second later he's there, appearing before me and making the women about me gasp. Yes, ladies—I know he's pretty. Keep it in your panties. I may not want that oversized penis inside *my* vagina right now, but I'm not too thrilled about the idea of it being nestled in any of *theirs*, either.

But his eyes are black, and a few of the women have the good mind to take a few steps back. They know who he is, even if the Sun Gods *are* elusive. We all do, and as far as these women are aware, he's as much to blame for our lifestyles as the Lord Almighty is. Right now, he certainly fucking looks the part.

I know why, too. He's been listening to my internal dialogue. He's pissed. But our very own Lord Almighty, King of the World has warded the Sun Gods against doing anything publicly that could spark a rebellion.

It would kill them.

Aero can't do anything to stop me. He certainly can't take me away amidst a crowd of people, whether I have time left on my one-hour wish ticker or not. They wouldn't risk their lives, the sun cycle, for the likes of a single Lesser Fae, because that would be risking the lives of every other being on this world.

And that's not them.

They're more than that.

They're bigger than that.

They have to be.

Aero lets out a low rumble as his canines lengthen, and I know I'm right.

'I'm sorry, Aero. I'm not doing this to hurt you …'

He looks positively sinister, like the master of pain these women probably suspect him to be. But he held me when I almost froze to death and didn't once try and prod me with his giant penis without my permission.

He's growling louder, and a few men are starting to take notice—mumbling about the God of Dawn making an appearance in Grueling. That our town's *blessed* or some shit. Fucking idiots. No god in their right mind would bless this piss smeared shit hole.

Some of the girls are looking my way, noting Aero's attention on me no doubt and probably feeling sorry for me. They shouldn't. Not now, anyway. Though that's about to change.

I finger my box. The one in my pocket, perverts, not my actual box. But that *does* need a good fingering too, which will have to wait until I'm done being a crazy impulsive bitch.

One of the fucktards on the dais announces the girl's sins. Apparently she *did* cry during sex with a customer at the establishment, and now I'm really fucking livid.

But my box needs to be kept safe from prying eyes.

I pull it from my pocket, dip my body low, and place it on the ground beneath my skirt, then slowly rise. I'm not sure if Aero's listening, he's a goddamn god after all, and his attention seems to be split between me, the crowd, and the dais right now. But yeah, I give it a red-hot crack anyway.

'I wish for you to hide this box, to not show Kal, Sol, or Drake its contents, and to not look in there yourself. Do you understand?' I say this in my mind, because the God of Dawn can't be seen to be fraternising with vermin such as myself.

His eyes widen, and now *all* of his attention is on me. Fists clenched, nostrils flared. The muscles on his forearms tense and coil.

A warm wave washes over my skin, though he doesn't respond, just looks at me with that penetrating glare. I take three steps towards him, towards the dais at his back.

"What the fuck are you doing?" he whisper-yells to me when I pass.

What am I doing? Good question.

"Remembering who I am," I murmur, as I storm towards the dais like a badass bitch with an agenda. I can't stand by and watch this shit. Especially when this shit is my goddamn fault.

Surprisingly, the crowd parts for me, leaving a trail of murmurs in my wake. Most of them likely know me, have seen some of the scenes I've started in the past, and are probably hoping they get to see me naked and brutalised again while they pump their little chodes. Sickos. I make it to the steps, just as the bastard with the whip prepares to crack it across the girl's front.

"Stop! Give me her punishment!" I yell, which earns me a gasp from the crowd because women aren't allowed to speak out of turn. Though I doubt this crowd will celebrate me with simultaneous orgasms. I wish they would, the world would be a much happier place if all the men focused more on their sex game and less on brutalising women.

The one with the whip eyes me up and down before jerking his chin to another man on the stand, who takes three long strides towards me with a cocky swag. He picks me up by the neck and tosses me at the feet of the young girl.

Fucking ouch. Whose bright idea was this?

Choking out a breath, I look up in time to see Kroe in all his dark-haired glory, sauntering up the opposite side of the dais, blood red sash wrapped tightly around his middle.

Fuck. This really is not my day.

You're probably expecting someone old and ugly with a middle-aged spread. The reality is quite the opposite. Though he is middle-aged, he's like a jar of pickles; well fucking preserved. I take in his chiselled jaw, roguish black curls that are perfectly styled and shiny, and his wide shoulders. I dare a peep at his knowing brown eyes. Condescending fuckers.

He runs his tongue across his teeth then whispers something into the ear of the bastard with the whip, who nods. Kroe takes two more steps, leans down and picks me up by the back of my blouse. I hang before him, arms dangling, head lolling.

Ugh, I didn't miss this.

The smell of cigars and brandy washes over me, assaulting my senses. My nose itches. The arsehole's still dusty. I have a split-second warning before I sneeze all over his face.

Whoops.

He frowns and wipes away my nose jizz before throwing me back down with a sneer. "I'll allow it. Forty lashings. She'll take the girls punishment, as well as her own for speaking out of turn."

Fucking wanker. I should've double sneeze jizzed his face.

The girl's bonds are loosened to the murmurs of the crowd and she drops into a whimpering pile on the floor. She'll probably get stitched up again and be waist deep in cum and hairy ball sacks before the sun sets. Then she'll die of infection, because that blood seeping out of her smells a little funky.

Fuck my life. I wish I could cry at times like this. Instead, I'm up here looking like a crazy bitch with a death wish.

Two of the men lift me from the ground by my arms, fastening me into place between the two poles that I've always thought look like giant, erect shlongs. Perhaps that's what they're meant to look like, and having a woman strung between them and whipped to within an inch of her life gives these men some sick sense of satisfaction.

Perhaps if I hadn't been frightened of Aero's penis, I wouldn't be in this predicament. I know that's messed up logic, but my head's a bit jumbled right now because I'm about to be slashed open by a fucking cat o' nine. And I'm not stupid, I saw the look in Kroe's eyes; he's glad to see me. This public whipping will probably be the least of my worries.

My skirt is tugged off me and I roll my eyes. Why the fuck does everyone need to see my labia when they're just lashing my back?

I pan my vision over the crowd as my bonds are tightened. Not the sort that make my vagina purr with anticipation.

I make out Kal, Drake, and now Sol, just shy of the back of the crowd. Kal is pissed, Drake is pissed, and Sol looks fucking savage. Wow, are they worried about me? No, probably not, they're just stressing about their magic boost. I need to hurry up and get through the rest of these wishes so the men don't feel so goddamn tethered to me. Then I can run away, find my way to the Day Kingdom, steal a chunk of sparkly floor and finally make that little life for myself in the East.

That's if Kroe doesn't fuck me into oblivion for leaving, or cut off all my limbs and make me that swinging sex chair so his customers can continue to pump me full of semen. I shudder at the thought as they tear my blouse from my body and drop it on the ground at my feet.

The sobbing girl is led off the landing. I turn away, unable to look at her any longer. I know her days are numbered.

I look towards Aero, surrounded by circles of kneeling men and women praying to him, while watching my show unfold. One fist is clenched, the other white knuckled, holding my wooden box.

Actually, he's not moving ... at all. He looks like an Aero statue. A really fucking brutal one, eyes flooding black and features sharpening, moulding him into something that looks positively frightening.

My eyes slip past Drake, then Kal, unmoving, gorgeous godly statues, canines bared.

Suspicion overrides ...

I shift my gaze to Sol. Beads of sweat are tearing down his face, jaw locked, his entire body trembling.

It clicks.

He's not taking any chances; he's holding his brothers at bay, protecting them from battling against those god killing wards.

Fuck.

My chest wrap is unwound from my body, setting my breasts free. The cold nips my nips and the scent of arousal rises in the crowd.

Kroe bows low to Aero from his place on the dais, slowly rises, then leans in close to my ear. "They're all imagining fucking you while you hang here. Even the Gods bless your punishment." His breath smells like the sardines on toast he had for breakfast. I hate sardines. "As much as I detest it, I've missed your rebellious side Adeline. This fantasy's going to make me a fortune."

He pulls away and I catch the eye of Sol. He looks like he's about to blow a fucking artery as he stands there, straining with the force of holding his brothers at bay. But his eyes are wide, and he doesn't *just* look angry ... he looks *terrified*.

He's probably frightened he's going to lose his hold and his brothers will die, along with his meaning for existence.

Shit.

Yeah, ok. I fucked up.

Then it hits ... the whip. It cracks through the air so loudly it takes me a moment to register the pain, but once I do, fuck me, it bites like ten snakes and stings like a viper going through menopause, except worse. Much, much worse.

I grit my teeth as the next one lands lower on my back, feeling the warm spill of blood. This fucker's lethal. I've never shed blood on the second lashing before. I hope I survive this, so I can live to suck this guy's testicles, and by suck them I mean bite them the fuck off. They'll probably take my head for it, but whatever, I'm done with this shit.

Another one hits, and another, and another, and it's like an endless wave of fire lashing across my back, sending crimson droplets spraying about me like a cloud of blood.

The cheers of the crowd fade out and I lose all perception of time.

Managing to look up at one point, all I see are my Gods, who really, let's be honest, have treated me bloody well. They haven't done this to me, and I've spoken out of turn over a thousand times around them.

I should've trusted them more—then maybe I wouldn't be here right now. But then, that young girl would be here instead, and I'm back to the bloody start again.

Fuck me, I think this is going to kill me. If I survive this, it'll be a miracle.

And yup, I just peed myself.

I doubt any of them will want my vagina anymore. Sorry girl, I've failed you.

She doesn't answer me, and I don't blame her. She'll probably hate me forever now and refuse to give me orgasms. She can be a vindictive twat sometimes.

Just when I'm about to pass the fuck out, a warm wash swarms over my skin, and though the whip still bites like a bitch I no longer feel like my body's about to fall to pieces, because the pain is battling with this warm tingly sensation, like tiny hands massaging me all over my skin.

It's Drake, I know it is, trying to give me something to cling to. But that darkness is really fucking tempting. And it's hauling at my vision, blurring the edges and tugging at my conscience.

I'm *dying*.

Fuck.

I don't want this … I don't want to fucking *die*.

But my body does, it so badly wants to slip. It's like I'm climbing a ladder and I'm almost at the top, but my hand keeps sliding off the last wrung and sending me crashing to the ground. Kal must be messing with my head, preventing me from slipping into the darkness, along with his magic boost. I'm not sure whether I should smite him or thank him for it.

I sink my teeth into my bottom lip, causing warm blood to dribble down my chin as the whip continues to lash at my flayed skin.

Again. Again. Again.

My teeth sink deeper—anything to prevent me from screaming out for this to stop.

Aero gains an inch, Sol's face crumbling as a droplet of sweat beads down the tip of his nose, landing on the ground before him.

No … he'll die.

'Stop! Aero, please! I'm okay …'

His features sharpen. He knows I'm lying.

He knows just as well as I do, part of me is dying.

But he doesn't understand; I've been through worse. I've *lived* through worse. I *will* live through this. I have my girls, and I'm a fucking *survivor*.

The whipping subsides and my hands are unbound. I collapse into a pool of my own blood, hair splayed around me, curls of ruby glistening in the early morning glow.

I stare at them, unblinking.

I can't move.

I can barely breathe.

"Unless you want word to get back to King Sterling that your girls are playing up, you need to keep your bitches on a tighter leash," the bastard with the whip says.

Kroe clears his throat. "Consider it done."

He picks me up and it almost destroys me all over again. I let out some unladylike noises, sounding like a wounded animal as he jostles my body, carrying me down the stairs and through the silent crowd.

It occurs to me that my blood's staining his perfectly white top. The fucker will probably get off on that later, wank one out while he sniffs it or some shit.

He gets in real close to my ear, hoisting me up a little and making me heave in the process. "Do you know how many girls I've had whipped or brutalised over the past few weeks, Cupcake? Too many. Too fucking many. But I knew you'd eventually take the bait."

What. The. Actual. Fuck.

I groan.

I let my girls down.

I let my mother down.

I let everyone fucking down.

"And now I have you back. It's going to be just like old times, though with a difference, because all those men in the crowd today were practically gagging for your cunt, and I know you like it rough, don't you sweets?"

Fuck my life. Fuck my fucking life.

I'm drifting, and I pray to the four Sun Gods that I don't wake up again, because something tells me this isn't going to be like old times at all.

Something tells me it's going to be a lot fucking worse.

THE END OF BOOK ONE.

ACKNOWLEDGMENTS

Thank you, Mum and Dad. You are a pillar of support and have always urged me to follow my dreams. I never expected those dreams would compel me to write a story about a prostitute who has conversations with her vagina, but we'll ignore that finer detail. I know you are proud of me, and that's all that matters!

Mum, when I read you the first chapter of this book, you never once batted an eyelid at all the slippery vaginas, never once told me I should write something more pertinent. In fact, you proceeded to sit down and brainstorm the rest of the series with me while we laughed hysterically over highly inappropriate innuendo.

Thank you for making me feel validated every day of my life. Thank you for the countless hours you have spent helping me to polish my work. I couldn't have done this without you.

My darling husband—thank you for believing in me, for reminding me of my untapped potential ... I bet you never expected it would spurt onto the pages of a book in the form of a reverse harem, huh?! (Insert laughing face here) But in all seriousness, thank you for sticking it out with me.

Nana, thank you for inspiring me with your creativity, and for showing me how strong and independent a woman can be. I love you, and not a day goes by that I don't miss you.

Lauren, thank you for the hours you invested into helping me, not to mention holding my hand through the entire publishing process. Most importantly, thank you for laughing at my vulgar sense of humour and dishing it right back at me.

My amazing ARC group, thank you all for investing time into this series, and giving me such validation. You're all wonderful.

To everyone else who has supported me along this journey that has only just begun, thank you!

ABOUT THE AUTHOR

SARAH ASHLEIGH PARKER

Sarah is New Zealand born and lives in the Gold Coast, Australia with her husband and their three children. She discovered her love for the written word early on, devouring book after book and creating her own stories in her spare time, winning various competitions throughout her school years for her quirky imagination.

It's only recently that she has been able to fully immerse herself into writing, being at home with three young children and an unquenchable thirst for creativity.

And so, with the timing being as good as it ever gets, and the passion and determination of a woman possessed, Sarah threw herself into becoming an author. Juggling an eclectic mix of manic writing, editing and proofing sessions, child rearing, homemaking and everything else life throws around, she somehow makes it work.

Sarah's preferred genre is dark adult fantasy romance and she has a large number of books in the works.

SPAWN OF DARKNESS SERIES

A Token's Worth
A Feather's Worth
A Lover's Worth
A Woman's Worth

A Feather's Worth

Spawn of Darkness

S.A. PARKER

A
LOVER'S
WORTH

Spawn of Darkness

S.A. PARKER

Printed in Great Britain
by Amazon